Taking Sonia's place had been easy...

Even so, when anyone called her Miss Frayne she wondered if she looked surprised.

Tina tried to relax. At least she was back in England. Through the crowd in the airport luggage area she saw Earle—her seatmate on the flight over—accompanied by a tall, arresting-looking man.

"Here's my friend Charles," said Earle, delightedly introducing them. "Charles, this is Miss Frayne...Sonia Frayne. We traveled together."

"Good lord, how odd!" was Charles Linton's unexpected greeting.

"That we should have traveled together?" Tina looked amused.

He regarded her with cool interest. Alarm bells suddenly clanged in Tina's head. "No," he said, "odd that your name should be Sonia Frayne. I think you are a cousin of mine."

Bargain Wife

by

MARY BURCHELL

Harlequin Books

TORONTO • LONDON • NEW YORK • AMSTERDAM
SYDNEY • HAMBURG • PARIS

Original hardcover edition published in 1979
by Mills & Boon Limited

This book, in a different version,
was originally published as *Where Shall I Wander?*

ISBN 0-373-02290-5

Harlequin edition published October 1979

Printed in U.S.A.

CHAPTER ONE

As Tina entered the hall of the apartment-block the cool of the air-conditioning fanned her face and she sighed with relief. It had been like that every evening for the last ten days. One thought nothing could be hotter than the walk from the Subway. Then that nothing could be hotter than the mean, sun-baked streets of this crowded bit of Brooklyn.

Three years ago—two years ago—perhaps even one year ago, Tina would have sought relief in deliberately recalling green fields in an English countryside, or London on a cool, grey, blowy day in autumn. Now she didn't dwell on memories of that kind. They hurt too much. Even more than the heat.

She climbed the stairs, pushed her key into the lock and opened the door of the little apartment she shared with Sonia. Here at least there was some sort of sanctuary.

'Hello!'

The girl who glanced up in casual greeting from her seat by the open window was wearing nothing but a cotton wrap in rather oppressively gay shades of yellow and red. Her legs dangled over the arm of the chair, and from her otherwise bare feet hung scarlet satin mules.

She was slim and hard and bright, from the crown of her slightly too blonde head to the tips of her scarlet toenails. But when she smiled—as she did now at Tina—her mouth widened in a not ungenerous curve, and her dark brown eyes sparkled attractively.

'Hot, isn't it?' murmured Tina absently.

'Original, aren't you?' retorted Sonia.

'Did the extra rehearsal go all right?'

'So-so.'

Tina laughed.

Sonia was a pianist who took any job available and had no illusions about the soloists whom it was her duty to accompany—or about anything else, come to that. Tina who at present played the violin with the same group, had few illusions, too, by now. The difference was that she had had them once and parted with them painfully. Sonia, starting with none, was incapable of being shocked and practically incapable of being hurt.

She was sorry for Tina when she thought about it. Probably her deepest and most real feeling was her affection for her friend. She knew that when Tina had come to the States three years ago she had cherished ideas of a life very different from the precarious, sordid existence which they picked up together playing where they could. Even Sonia, however—who had known Tina only during the last eighteen months—had no idea quite how bright those early hopes had been. She knew that Tina had been left an orphan at twenty-one, with little money, a sound musical education, and boundless optimism and faith in the future.

Why she should have supposed that a successful career awaited almost any talented musical student who had the good fortune to go to the United States, Sonia could never imagine. Anyway, whatever the reason, when Tina's parents had died, she had broken the few remaining links with her life in England, realised her tiny capital, and set out for the United States with highest hopes.

Nowadays, of course, even Tina realised that disaster and disillusionment had been inevitable. She was not a flaming genius—she would have been the last to claim that for herself—and she possessed not one scrap of influence. She was simply a talented, hard-working student. And of those there were already hundreds—even thousands.

Even to Sonia she had never fully described the rapid descent from dreams to reality, the inevitable passage from the elegant offices of polite but uninterested concert agents

to the not-so-elegant offices of impolite and all-too-much
interested theatrical agents of the shadier kind. Tina, who
had once thought in terms of concert platforms, found she
was exceedingly lucky if she could drag a living wage from
dubious week-to-week engagements.

When she had met Sonia, eighteen months ago, they had
both been applying for vacancies with a small backing
group in a nightclub—with an eagerness dictated more by
considerations of the next meal than by any enthusiasm for
the job as such. Both of them were lucky, as it happened,
and both entered on the first semi-permanent job they had
ever had.

After a few weeks they decided to pool their small re-
sources and share an apartment, and probably this oddly
assorted companionship was the first thing that had brought
any solid satisfaction to Tina since she had left England.
She was fond of Sonia—who was unscrupulous but somehow likeable—and if their philosophies of life could hardly
have been more different, a certain honesty of outlook—
cynical in Sonia and idealistic in Tina—cemented any
cracks in the surface of their day-to-day life.

Without preamble, Sonia announced suddenly:

'If old Cyrus Manton asks me to go away with him, I
shall.'

Characteristically she asked for no advice—merely stated
a decision.

Tina's eyes opened wide, in spite of the fact that she was
now more or less used to her friend's uncompromising view
of life.

'Sonia! He's so—so *old*!' she exclaimed, knowing instinctively that it was useless to argue the moral issue.

'Old enough to be a sugar daddy,' countered Sonia
cynically. 'Much the sugariest daddy who is ever likely to
come my way.'

Tina regarded her friend in anxious perplexity.

'Sonia, it isn't worth it.'

'What isn't worth what?' Sonia wanted to know.

'Oh, the—luxury and the freedom from money worries

aren't worth the—the loss of self-respect and——'

'It's different for you, honey.' Sonia regarded her not unkindly. 'You're all simple and sweet and English still.'

'It's nothing to do with being English,' Tina protested. 'And come to that, you're English yourself.'

Sonia laughed.

'Only technically. You can't count the first two years of your life as meaning anything. I'm more American than the Americans now. But anyway, as you say, it's not any question of nationality. It's a question of butter on your bread—and a slice of pecan pie too,' she added with a grin.

Tina smiled, but gravely, because she was still concerned with the essential point of Sonia's decision.

'Anyway, he may not ask you,' she said hopefully at last.

'Wish me luck,' Sonia retorted wickedly.

'You're having supper with him tonight?'

'I am. And if any suggestions are coming along, they'll be made then.'

They were both silent for a moment. Then Tina said in an abstracted way:

'I shall miss you.'

'It isn't settled yet,' Sonia replied quickly, with a little flash of superstition that was her one weakness. 'It doesn't do to count on a thing until it's sure.'

'No,' Tina said. But in her heart she thought with sudden conviction, 'I *am* sure. Something is going to take Sonia away from me and I shall be alone again.'

'Come along. Hurry!' Sonia's voice broke in a little impatiently on her reverie. 'It's gone half-past. If we don't want to run all the way to the Subway we must make a move. It won't do to be late tonight. If Louis has anything to complain of besides the heat, he isn't going to be too nice to know.'

Acknowledging the truth of that—for the leader of their group was not an easy taskmaster—Tina changed with a slick expertness which Sonia had taught her, and pronounced herself ready.

As they left the building together, the two girls might

well have been taken for sisters. Both of them were almost startlingly fair—though Sonia was distinctly fairer than Nature had intended her to be—almost identical in height, both with the same slim, trim type of figure which comes from never having quite enough to eat, but never going quite so hungry that the fact advertises itself. Sonia's eyes were a bright, clear brown—Tina's, soft and velvety; and while Sonia looked at the world with a cool and uncompromising stare, Tina's wide eyes still held something of the soft, inquiring expression of a good child, who almost believes that things will go right but fears just a little that they may go all wrong.

On the journey to town Tina deliberately tried to make her mind blank. She was already tired and dispirited with the heat and rush of the day, and she didn't want to think about *anything* at the moment. Particularly she didn't want to think about this startling decision of Sonia's.

At the back of her mind, however, there remained a persistent, aching anxiety, partly on account of Sonia herself and partly because of the effect this new move would have on her own life. It would mean a new style of living—for it would be impossible to keep on even their tiny flat on her own salary—a new loneliness, and a new lack of security. The cool, bright, hard presence of Sonia *had* given a sense of security—if only because of the consciousness that few things, if any, could nonplus her.

'Don't be so disgustingly selfish,' Tina told herself. 'It's Sonia's life that is likely to be ruined—not yours.'

But somehow the words carried no conviction, even to herself.

When she reached home alone that night the first thing she noticed was a letter lying on the mat. Not just *a* letter —an ordinary letter—but a letter which, most surprisingly and excitingly, bore an English stamp.

Tina snatched it up, then saw that the letter was addressed to Sonia.

She stood quite still in the centre of the room, staring at the envelope. The address was unmistakable—'Miss Sonia

Frayne.' And it had been addressed to the house where Sonia had lodged before she and Tina joined forces. Some-one had readdressed it here.

Unquestionably it was Sonia's letter—and absolutely no business of Tina's. But it was all she could do to make her mind accept the fact that a letter from England—*England!* —could belong to Sonia and not to herself. Why, it was more than twenty years since Sonia had been brought to the States. She had been a baby—there was no connection left between her and the country of her birth. In all the while Tina had known her she had never received a letter with an English stamp and postmark.

With some idea of keeping her thoughts away from it, she carefully avoided looking at the letter again. And, even when she was in bed, she took a book and read steadily— partly with the idea of remaining awake until Sonia re-turned, and partly because she knew suddenly that if she lay still in the darkness the presence of that letter would evoke memories and regrets that were very nearly unbearable.

It was three o'clock before she heard the light sound of Sonia's feet running up the last flight of stairs.

She must have had an exhilarating time if she felt like running upstairs at this hour, thought Tina subconsciously, and she sat up as the door opened.

'Oh—you're awake still.' There was a dash of bright but perfectly natural colour in Sonia's cheeks, and her elabor-ately casual manner did nothing to hide the fact that she was tremendously excited about something.

'Yes, of course. Did you—did you have a good time?'

'Splendid, thanks.'

'Did—things go as you wanted?'

'If you mean "as I expected"—no.'

'Then——'

'Tina, take a deep breath and hold on tight to some-thing. Cyrus Manton—one of the richest men on Wall Street—has asked me to marry him.'

Tina took the deep breath, not before the statement but after it—and she took it in one great gasp.

'To *marry* you?—him, I mean. It's impossible!'

'No, it's not impossible. I've been telling myself that all the way home. But it's not impossible, it's a fact. It's half done already.' And unable, with all her casualness, to hide a certain sense of triumph, she held out her left hand, on which there winked and sparkled quite the biggest diamond Tina had ever seen.

'Then you—accepted?' Tina said rather stupidly.

'Accepted? *Accepted!* Darling girl, who do you suppose is going to refuse diamond-studded security for the rest of her life?'

'A lifetime seems an awful while to spend with Cyrus Manton,' Tina couldn't help saying rather sombrely.

'I shan't have to spend a lifetime with him.' Sonia was impatiently callous. 'He's sixty-five now, if he's a day. Even if he lives to eighty—and his overworked sort seldom do—I shall still be under forty when I become one of the richest widows in America.'

Tina winced a little, in spite of the fact that she was so used to Sonia's way of regarding things.

'There's a letter for you, Sonia—from England,' she changed the subject.

'From England?' Sonia didn't even glance at it. 'Aunt Maggie, I suppose. She remembers me every five years or so.'

'It's typewritten.'

'Is it?' Sonia was interested momentarily, and getting up from the end of Tina's bed, where she had been sitting, she picked up the letter and slit open the envelope—pausing as she did so to admire her ring afresh.

'I bet he didn't get that under ten thousand dollars,' she remarked with satisfaction as she drew out the letter.

She read for a moment in silence, and then drew in her breath in a soft, amused whistle.

'How odd!' She sat down on Tina's bed again, laughing a little. 'A few months ago I'd have thought this a gift from heaven. Now it doesn't even matter, not worth worrying about. Listen, Tina. It's a letter from some lawyers. My

Aunt Maggie's pegged out, poor old thing—though, as I've never seen her since I was eighteen months old, I can't be expected to be heartbroken. Anyway, she's left me her all. About a thousand pounds, these people seem to think.'

Tina was far more impressed by this than by any offer of marriage from Cyrus Manton.

'Funny, isn't it? I suppose that would about pay for half a dozen dresses for Mrs Cyrus Manton. It isn't worth collecting now, Tina.' Sonia laughed. 'No, no, no! Mrs Cyrus Manton has something better to do than go all that way just for that.'

'Go there, Sonia? Go to *England*! With a thousand pounds waiting there for you! Oh, what heaven! What absolute heaven! You *can't* want to marry that fat old Manton man now!'

Sonia stared at her incredulously.

'What on earth are you talking about? What's a thousand pounds in England—or anywhere else for that matter—compared with being the wife of a millionaire?'

'Oh, but'—Tina was twisting her hands together with the intensity of her feelings—'but *England*! To go back home——' Suddenly she began to cry.

A good deal moved in spite of herself, Sonia came and put her arm round Tina.

'Well, don't cry about it. It isn't worth crying about—at least, I suppose it is to you. That's the difference—things mean a whole lot more to you. Well then, *you* have the thousand or whatever it is. You go home to England and pretend to be me. I'll get my old man to give you the ticket home as one of my wedding presents. Yes'—she was pleased with the idea of testing her future husband's generosity so speedily—'that's a grand idea. You can have my old passport to establish your identity or whatever is needed. I shan't want it any more. You take it.'

Tina interrupted, laughing a little through her tears.

'Oh, Sonia, you're a darling. But you mustn't play about with passports like that. It's—it's a punishable offence, I'm sure.'

'Who's to punish who? I'll have a joint passport with my husband now, because we're going on a flying trip to Buenos Aires on our honeymoon. It's all settled. You're quite enough like the photograph in my old passport. You go home to England, Tina, and take that with you. Collect the old thousand and then fade out into any part of your blessed island that you fancy. You aren't made for this sort of life—I know it as well as you. If poor old Aunt Maggie only knew, she'd be a lot better pleased that the money went to a nice, good little thing like you than to a gold-digger who paints her toenails. So it's the right thing from any point of view.'

'But'—Tina hugged Sonia suddenly—'there must be a better way of arranging it, Sonia. I'm not going to turn all proud and self-respecting and refuse—because I simply can't. The thought of going home—and going home to some sort of fresh start—makes me nearly crazy with joy and relief. But I can't do this impersonation act, dear. It's quite impossible. Can't you—can't you arrange some legal transfer—or—or deed of gift or something? Surely one can do these things.'

But Sonia's interest began to wane at once.

'But, my dear little idiot, there isn't time. Oh, I didn't tell you—I'm being married tomorrow. At least, it's to-morrow now'—she glanced absently at her watch. 'We're leaving on the afternoon plane for the south, and afterwards we go on to Buenos Aires. Cyrus (isn't it a frightful name when you say it by itself?) has business there. I've no idea when we'll be back. There's no time for anything but to shop and get married. I can't go running round to lawyers, getting deeds settled.' Characteristically, she was not willing to back up a generous impulse by taking any personal trouble. 'You can have the money and welcome, my dear, but much the simplest way is to take the passport too. You'll find it in that drawer over there.'

'Sonia, *please*'—Tina was trembling with eagerness, and she gripped Sonia's arm with nervous fingers—'won't you do it the other way? It doesn't matter about doing it before

you leave New York. You can do it from Florida or
wherever you're going in the south. You can send it to me
—the deed or letter, I mean. I wouldn't need it for a week
or two anyway, because I've got to work out my notice and
arrange everything else. Do say "yes", Sonia. I could go
mad with happiness at the thought of your generosity, and
if you would just arrange things this way, everything would
be all right.'

'All right.' Sonia gave her a quick, rare kiss. 'You can go
mad with a clear conscience. I'll see you have your old
document, signed, sealed, and everything else. I'll send it
from the very first place where we stop long enough.'

CHAPTER TWO

THE next thirty-six hours developed into a hectic rush of arranging, rearranging, shopping, and trying on of bewilderingly beautiful clothes. Sonia's future husband seemed to set no limit to the amount of money he was willing to spend on her, and Sonia, as she said, saw no reason why she should not gratify that particular wish of his to the furthest limits.

Tina was not quite sure whether she herself was more scandalised or amused to see the amount of cold cash which Sonia had already contrived to extract from her admirer.

Over breakfast she produced a wad of notes and slapped them down triumphantly beside her plate.

'First dividend,' she informed Tina with a smile.

And when Tina said a little dryly, 'Quick work, isn't it?' Sonia simply opened her big brown eyes very wide and protested:

'Oh, but *why*? If he wants to marry me, I suppose he wants me to do him credit at the wedding. And if he wants me to do him credit at the wedding, I suppose he knows there's only one person who can provide the cash. And if he *is* going to provide it, where's the sense in wasting time?'

'It sounds very simple, put that way,' Tina agreed with a smile. 'Is that how you argued it to him?'

But Sonia shook her head.

'Oh no. I believe in starting as I'm going on,' she explained crisply. 'I just came straight to the point and said, "It'll take a heap of money to make me look the part," and he reached for his pocket-book at once. He knew what I meant.'

Tina wondered how he could have failed to do so.

Sonia, she noticed, extracted considerable malicious pleasure from the consternation of Louis, their employer, when she announced her immediate resignation and offered no explanation other than that she was getting married.

When Tina in her turn—and rather more timidly—tendered her month's notice, Louis regarded her with those uncomfortably penetrating light eyes of his, which never altered their expression even when he smiled.

'Another wedding?' he inquired cynically.

'No,' Tina said. 'No, I'm—going back home.'

'To England?'

'Yes, to England.'

Sonia's marriage—unlike anything Tina had ever thought a wedding should be—came as a strange climax to a strange couple of days. The short, unromantic ceremony at City Hall made Tina somehow oddly embarrassed. And not all her painfully acquired sophistication was equal to the strain of watching unmoved while Sonia took on the rôle of an old man's darling without so much as a flicker of her mascaraed eyelashes.

However, Tina's reflections were of no importance, of course, and certainly there was no question but that Sonia herself was completely satisfied. She looked radiant, and already adopted towards her elderly bridegroom an air of smiling confidence which showed she had no misgivings about how she intended to play her new rôle.

Later, at the superb champagne luncheon which they all three shared at Manhattan's most exclusive hotel, she accepted the luxurious surroundings, the homage of the head waiter, the extravagant devotion of her new husband, as though she had been used to these things all her life. No one, seeing her now, reflected Tina admiringly, could dream that she was nothing but an unsuccessful musician, used to cooking her own inadequate meals in a poky Brooklyn apartment.

Determined that Tina should share as many of the new

thrills as possible, Sonia insisted that she came down with them to the airport in the shining, streamlined Cadillac.

'Merton can drive you back to town after we're gone,' she added casually, as though giving her orders to a chauffeur who had always been part of her daily routine.

'Thank you,' murmured Tina—a little inadequately she felt, and for the first time it was really borne in on her that this was 'goodbye' to Sonia. For eighteen months they had shared almost every detail of their everyday life, and now they were most unlikely ever to see each other again.

Sonia, unable to think of anything but the excitement of her new existence, was not wasting any sentimental regrets, Tina knew. But she herself—happy though she was at the thought of her journey to England—could not see the links snapping without a tightening of her throat. Aloud she said:

'Perhaps you'll come to Europe some day, Sonia.'

'Oh, of course,' Sonia agreed cheerfully.

'I make the trip every year,' interjected her husband at this moment, and Tina reflected that it was almost the only sentence he had addressed to her—even in this oblique fashion. Evidently he had less than no interest in his young wife's one-time associates.

However, it seemed that Sonia had not counted in vain on his extending his generosity to cover Tina's needs. For when the hurried goodbyes were said—while it seemed to Tina that the impatient hum of the waiting plane added the last touch of fantasy to the scene—she thrust a thick envelope into Tina's hand.

'There you are, honey. Call it the bridegroom's present to his bridesmaid, if you like. It'll buy your ticket to England—and I hope you enjoy yourself when you get there.'

'Oh, Sonia! Dear, dear Sonia—thank you.'

Tina wanted to say much more. She felt that all the words in the world were not enough to describe her relief and gratitude. But anyway, there was no time to say them now. Sonia was hugging her with unwonted warmth and they were kissing each other goodbye, while Cyrus Manton looked on rather sombrely, as though he grudged this slight display of affection on his wife's part, even though it was directed to such a harmless recipient as Tina.

'I'll send you that letter the very first moment I have,' Sonia promised. 'We're stopping off at Miami for a day or two, and I'll do it then. Goodbye.'

'Goodbye, Sonia. And thank you for everything.'

No millionairess by birth could have accepted the thanks more charmingly as her due, and as Sonia followed her husband to the plane, Tina thought:

'She's stepping right into her new life—word-perfect from the beginning.'

It seemed only a matter of seconds then before the doors of the plane were shut and the machine was roaring across the field, clumsily at first and then incredibly gracefully as it gathered speed.

She waved, because that seemed the right thing to do, and no doubt Sonia could see her for a few moments from the window. But almost immediately the plane became a distant speck against the clouds, and the voice of Cyrus Manton's chauffeur—*Sonia's* chauffeur—was saying respectfully behind her:

'Where did you want me to take you, miss?'

During the drive back to town Tina decided not to go back to the empty apartment. She would stay up in town— have a meal before going home. She could afford it now. She could afford to allow herself a few luxuries. Nothing stupidly extravagant, of course, just something to mark the difference between the sordid struggle of yesterday and the brightness of tomorrow.

She hardly minded the usual discomforts and annoyances of the nightclub that evening. Louis was in a specially trying mood—possibly because the hastily acquired substitute for Sonia was anything but satisfactory. But Tina felt impervious to irritation. In a little while she would be gone.

When she was changing to go home, she felt very

sharply the realisation that Sonia was gone from her life. It would be quiet and lonely in the Brooklyn apartment, and she hoped with genuine fervour that it would not be long before her arrangements for her journey could be completed.

As she came out of the back exit from the club, the thunderstorm which had been threatening for days broke in sudden fury. Lightning flashed overhead, and the rain was driven in long, piercing spearheads down the narrow street which seemed now like a dark canyon, sunk between the tall buildings on either side.

With an exclamation Tina stepped back again into the doorway, sheltering from the first heavy downpour. It would not last long like this. She would wait for a few minutes before running for her subway station.

As she stood there she idly watched the newspaper man at the opposite corner, sheltering under his streaming tarpaulin, already doing a brisk trade in the morning's papers.

At that moment a damp, flapping placard flattened itself out against the newspaper stall, and Tina read, with a sort of horrid fascination which printed every word on her mind:

'WALL STREET MAGNATE DIES IN PLANE CRASH.'

Without thinking now of the rain she dashed across the road. Her fingers trembled so much that she could hardly find the money to pay for the damp paper which she snatched from the man's hand.

But she scarcely needed to read the words which ran across two columns of the front page. She was fatalistically aware of them almost before she saw them:

'Cyrus Manton perishes in blazing plane. ... No survivors.... Several passengers still unidentified ...'

They were dead. Sonia and that old man who was going to give her everything she wanted were dead. All that bright, demanding Sonia had got out of that opportunity she thought so marvellous was limitless anticipation.

Swaying backwards and forwards with the motion of the subway train, Tina tried to fix her thoughts on first one and then another aspect of the situation, but it seemed as though her thoughts, too, swayed backwards and forwards, refusing to attach themselves for more than a minute to any one thing.

More by chance than anything else she noticed that she had arrived at her station, and got out of the train just before it started to move again. On the short walk to the apartment she was still thinking:

'Sonia is gone.... But you didn't ever expect to see her again anyway.... No, but that's different. She's dead. That's different.... But there was going to be half the world between you in a week or two. You're going home to England and——'

With a start that really made her feel physically ill, Tina suddenly arrived at the most frightful realisation of all. She *couldn't* go home to England now, after all. *Her* wonderful chance was gone too. She had the price of her ticket in her bag, it was true, but there was nothing—and no one—waiting for her the other side. Not a thing. Not a prospect —not a penny. At one time she would have hoped eagerly for the best and taken the risk. But the years of sickening, futile searching for jobs had sapped her confidence. She couldn't go back now. Her chance was gone.

She didn't sit down when she got in. She walked up and down the strangely silent and empty room.

'It can't be true. It simply can't be true,' she kept on telling herself. 'Sonia meant me to have that money— that chance. With all her heart she meant it. It's lying there in some bank, or some lawyer's safe—waiting for me to claim it—that thousand pounds that means everything. There *must* be some way——'

Suddenly she stopped in her walk, her eyes wide and dark in her unusually pale face, her whole air suggestive of someone who was listening.

Like a voice from the past—so really and tragically the past now—Sonia's words seemed to sound again:

'You can have my old passport to establish your identity. Go home to England, Tina, and take that with you. You'll find it in that drawer over there.'

Slowly, as though not moving quite of her own volition, Tina crossed the room and pulled open a drawer.

It was there—just as Sonia had said—the passport back to all that mattered. Fascinatedly she turned the pages and looked at the photograph. Not much like Sonia—sufficiently unlike for one to be able to look at it without a pang of memory.

If she did her hair that way the superficial likeness would be much more striking.

Then the description. Hair—blonde. Eyes—brown. Height—five feet four. It fitted.

'It's a criminal offence, of course,' Tina murmured aloud but absently, as though that part of the idea hardly interested her.

Specimen signature. Sonia's round, schoolgirlish handwriting would not be difficult to copy. With a little practice——

Sitting down at the table, Tina took out her fountainpen. Slowly at first and with care, then gradually with more confidence and natural speed—she wrote one name over and over again.

Sonia Frayne. Sonia Frayne. Sonia Frayne.

It was unusually late when Tina woke the next morning, and she lay there in bed for a few moments wondering why she felt depressed, yet excited. Then the overwhelming consciousness that she was alone in the room reminded her, in one tremendous rush, of all that had happened last night.

Raising herself on her elbow, she glanced round the room, rather as though she imagined she must see Sonia asleep in the other bed—very bright and concrete, a living refutation of the fantastic imaginings of the last few hours.

But there was no Sonia. The other bed remained somewhat aggressively in the 'chair' state—pushed against the wall. And far the most significant—and, in a way, frightening—thing in the room was the untidy jumble of paper on the table, sheet after sheet of which had been covered with a copy of Sonia's handwriting.

Jumping out of bed, Tina swept the sheets together. There was nowhere where she could burn them, and yet the very thought of their being sent down the rubbish-chute intact—a dreadful and significant witness against her—made her swallow nervously.

Already, she supposed with a sort of fascinated dismay, she was a criminal covering her tracks.

Then she determinedly forced herself to see things in more reasonable proportion. She was not being a criminal. She was carrying out the very thing which Sonia wanted done. There was no one to suffer by it. An irregular way of managing things, of course, but not morally a crime. In fact——

But, all the same, those papers must be destroyed.

Taking them to the small sink in the kitchen, she put a match to them, watched them burn, and washed the ashes down the drain. Then she collected her newspaper from the letter-box, and over her scanty breakfast she read again the details of the dramatic accident.

There was no doubt, it seemed, about Cyrus Manton himself having been on the plane. His seat had been booked several days ago.

'I expect,' thought Tina, 'it was the idea of going away that made him finally ask Sonia to go with him. And her ticket would be taken at the last minute, of course, because he wouldn't know until then that she was really going.'

A famous film star, it was now known, had also been a passenger, and that was enough in itself to throw the unnamed and unknown occupants completely in the shade. They were classed together with tragic indifference as 'three, if not four, other passengers, whose identity is as yet unknown.'

'*As yet*,' Tina reminded herself warningly. 'Anything may come out yet. The chauffeur may know more than I supposed and talk. Someone at the register office may scent a news story.' Though she remembered now, for the first time, how nervous and uncertain the official who had performed the brief ceremony had been. She had thought at the time, 'New to the job, poor thing,' and Sonia had been faintly annoyed because he obviously had no idea that the elderly bridegroom was a person of some importance.

But there were so many pitfalls to last night's half-formed project that, by now, the whole thing seemed quite impossible to carry out. She need not agitate herself so much about whether her idea were criminal or not. She was extremely unlikely ever to have the chance of testing it.

In a way, that was almost a relief, she thought. Then she remembered, with a desperate, angry feeling of frustration, that if she *could* not carry it out, her way of escape was closed. No return to England for her. Just Louis and the club and New York for what seemed like ever and ever and ever.

It was a very sober and thoughtful Tina who joined the other members of the group for rehearsal that morning, and it seemed uncanny to her that no one—*no* one—mentioned the momentous fact that Sonia was dead.

How could they, of course?—since they had no idea of the fact. And yet it seemed impossible that this thing should have happened and none of her associates know the fact. Anxious though she was to keep a check on her own tongue, Tina found herself, more than once, on the very verge of saying something which would have betrayed what she now regarded as her guilty knowledge.

And when Louis mentioned Sonia quite casually, it was all she could do not to betray her extreme agitation. To be sure, his inquiry was conventional enough. Just a slightly sneering:

'Has our bright and beautiful Sonia departed on her wedding trip yet?'

'Yes,' Tina said carefully, trying not to think of herself waving goodbye to Sonia not twenty-four hours ago. 'Yes, she went off yesterday.'

'Was she going far?' Louis was not really interested, beyond a casual curiosity, and even as he spoke, he was turning over sheets of music. But Tina passed the tip of her tongue over her dry lips, because this was the moment for her first lie, if she were to tell it.

'Out West somewhere, I think.' She was amazed to hear how her own casual tone matched Louis's. 'But you know how secretive Sonia could be. She didn't talk much to me about it.'

'Did you see the husband?' Louis was frankly curious, though not, of course, in the slightest degree suspicious. He had no reason to be.

'I—yes.' Tina gave the truthful reply unthinkingly, though the next moment she wished she had denied all knowledge of him. It would have been much the safest thing.

'What was he like?' Louis glanced up from the music he was examining.

'Oh—a good deal older than she was. But I should say he had plenty of money to spend on her, and was willing to spend it.'

Louis laughed cynically again.

'Just suit our little Sonia,' he remarked. 'A gold-digger born and bred. And a gold-digger she'll be until the day she dies.'

Tina said nothing. She turned away. But she felt that Sonia's epitaph had unquestionably been spoken.

When she came out of the club from rehearsal someone touched her arm and said, 'Excuse me, miss,' and turning back quickly, she found Cyrus Manton's chauffeur standing at her elbow.

For a moment she supposed her sensations were not unlike those of an escaped prisoner when a policeman touches him on the arm. Then she recovered herself, and with the resigned admission that things were now taken out of her hands, she said:

'Yes? What is it?'

'Have you an hour to spare, miss? There's someone who wants to see you rather urgently.'

'Wants to see *me*?' She was completely bewildered. Her first idea had been that he wanted to make himself a nuisance. But of course he could not have any inkling of any intentions *she* had had of impersonating Sonia. And, in any case, his manner was entirely inoffensive. Much more persuasive than threatening, she couldn't help thinking. 'But who wants to see me?' she asked curiously.

He hesitated a moment. Then he said:

'It was Mrs Manton that sent me.'

'Mrs Manton!' For a wild moment she wondered if Sonia had escaped from that plane wreck. Then the man said:

'The first Mrs Manton, if you understand me, miss.'

Tina remembered the former wife mentioned in that long obituary notice then, and said that she understood him.

'But why does she want to see *me*?' Tina wanted to know.

'Perhaps you'd best let her explain that herself,' the man said respectfully but quite firmly. And after a moment's thought Tina made up her mind.

'All right, I'll come.'

'The car's round here,' the man told her, and led her into a side street, where there stood the sleek, shining Cadillac in which they had all driven out to the airport only yesterday.

Partly because she wanted to question the man and partly because of an instinctive distaste for sitting where she had sat yesterday, she sat in front with the chauffeur.

They drove in silence for a few minutes. Then he said:

'You'll have heard of the accident, of course?'

'Yes,' Tina said. 'I heard about it last night. It's a—dreadful business, isn't it?'

'Yes, miss.'

'When did you hear about it?' she asked, after a minute.

'This morning. Mrs Manton telephoned for me. She'd read the news in the morning's paper and knew I'd have been the last to see him. She wanted to know if I could tell her why he was on that particular plane, and so on.'

Again there was a slight pause. Then Tina said:

'Did you—tell her?'

'About Mr Manton marrying again, you mean?' The man was evidently no fool. 'Yes, I told her. That's why she wanted to see you.'

'I don't—quite see the connection.'

'You and me were the witnesses,' the man said cryptically. 'Here we are, miss.' And the car drew up outside one of the big houses on Riverside Drive which Tina had often passed but never expected to enter.

He got out and rang the bell for her, but it seemed he was not coming in with her, because as soon as the door was opened he simply said to the manservant: 'This is the young lady that's expected,' and then went back to the car.

Tina felt slightly nervous but intensely curious as she followed the servant through a long, flower-filled hall to a room at the end. He opened the door for her but made no sort of announcement, and Tina went forward into a lofty, light room, furnished with incredible richness. She had no time to notice details, but the overwhelming impression of luxury was like nothing else she had ever experienced. And the woman who rose to her feet at once as she entered was as beautifully dressed as anyone Tina had ever seen outside a film.

She was in black—but whether as a tribute to the late Cyrus Manton or her own dazzling fairness, Tina would not have liked to say—and as she moved, her dress seemed to be part of her. She smiled too, graciously, but rather with that graciousness which exalts the dispenser and abashes the recipient. Evidently there was little doubt in her mind where to place Tina in the social scale.

'My dear, do come in and sit down. I understand you are the special friend of—of the young woman who was killed with my husband yesterday. I wanted so much to speak to you. It must have been a frightful shock for you, this accident.'

'Why, yes,' Tina agreed gently, 'it was. But it must have been a great shock for you too.'

'Yes, it *was* a shock for me too, of course. Though my husband and I had not been seeing much of each other for the last three years. But we were very good *friends*, you understand.'

Tina murmured something to indicate that she understood this peculiar state of affairs exactly.

'But do tell me about your poor young friend. She had been seeing quite a lot of my husband, hadn't she?'

'She was married to him,' Tina stated bluntly, seeing no reason why they should circle round the point any longer. 'I thought you knew that.'

'Yes, of course. Merton did *mention* a ceremony of some sort yesterday.' This was murmured regretfully as though they were discussing a luncheon engagement which had rather unexpectedly occurred. 'I understand that you and he were the witnesses.'

'Yes.'

'And no one else was present?'

'No,' Tina said. 'No one else was there.' She felt her breath beginning to come rather quickly. Was it possible that this woman was going to play straight into her hands?

'Had she any family, this friend of yours?—any relations in this country?'

'None at all.' Tina said that quite calmly and looked at the late Cyrus Manton's wife very frankly.

'Poor child! How *sad*!' Mrs Manton exclaimed almost genially. She was quite unable to conceal her relief under a decent cloak of sympathy. 'Then she was quite alone?— except for you, of course. Simply *no* one to be interested in what happened to her?'

'No one,' Tina agreed deliberately.

'I *see*.' Mrs Manton spoke as though an entirely new aspect of the case had suddenly occurred to her. She even got up from her seat and walked up the long room and back again.

Then she stopped in front of Tina with almost dramatic suddenness.

'Do you know—I've just been wondering if it wouldn't

be better—I mean, it isn't as though there's anything in it to *harm* the poor girl's memory or anything——'

She paused, as though lost in thought, and Tina, feeling faintly embarrassed that this little comedy for saving Mrs Manton's face was so dreadfully transparent to her, cut through the tangle of pretence.

'Are you trying to say that—for various reasons—it might be better that this marriage of your husband's should remain a secret?'

'Well, you know, the idea did just *occur* to me as we were talking.' ('Liar,' thought Tina dispassionately.) 'You see—I don't expect you've had much to do with lawyers and lawyers' fees. But I *have*. And in a case where there is any dispute about a big estate—well, my dear, they take everything. But simply *everything*. There's practically nothing left for the wretched beneficiaries.' And she flung out her hands dramatically to emphasise the degree of poverty to which she would probably be reduced.

'Not to mention the first Mrs Manton,' thought Tina with grim amusement. 'I suppose she would have heroics about it too. Not that I have any right to criticise them,' she reminded herself ruthlessly the next moment. 'They're no better—and no worse—than I am. It suits every single one of us that Sonia's disappearance should go unnoticed. I feel awful to be concerned in this. But then what is there that I should—or could—do about it? It's not as though there are the rights of anyone else to be protected.'

She became aware that Mrs Manton was watching her with an anxiety which was completely undisguised by her studied air of considering the whole question simply on its merits.

'Mrs Manton,' Tina said slowly, 'if you see no reason to make public your husband's secret third marriage, I don't think anyone else will. I have no reason to talk about Sonia either.' (If this woman only knew how she had every reason *not* to!) 'I'm terribly, terribly sorry that this dreadful thing happened to her. But, as a matter of fact, I felt I'd probably said goodbye to her in any case. I'm going back to England myself in a few weeks' time, and I was very unlikely to meet her again. Certainly not for some years.'

'But how fort—— that is, *interesting* !' Mrs Manton swiftly recovered herself. 'And—do tell me—were there any other friends of hers who knew about this romantic marriage?'

'There was no one,' Tina said quietly. 'Of that I'm absolutely certain. She was only engaged for a couple of days and she—she was rather anxious to leave all her old life behind, you know.'

'Of course, of course.' This was evidently a sentiment with which the other Mrs Manton could sympathise. 'Then you and Merton——'

'Are the only people to know about it. Unless, of course, Mr Manton himself mentioned it to anyone.'

'Most unlikely,' stated his widow firmly, evidently drawing on some special knowledge she had of him. 'And Merton, of course, is so very, very discreet. Besides,' she added with apparent irrelevance, 'he's so *very* fond of his little cottage on the Connecticut estate.'

'Then it seems you have nothing to worry about, doesn't it?' Tina said, concealing a certain degree of amusement.

'Oh, I wasn't *worried* about anything,' Mrs Manton assured her, with a sweet, low-pitched laugh. 'I only wanted so much to do what was best for *everyone*. And you've helped me so much, my dear. And I'm so interested in this journey of yours to England. If there is any way in which I can help you—I mean, I do know travelling is so *expensive*, and when a girl is earning her own living——'

'That's very kind of you, but there's nothing—really nothing—that I need,' Tina assured her with great firmness. And she rose to go.

For some reason or other she experienced a terrible revulsion of feeling at this hardly veiled offer of money. To take what Sonia had meant her to have, even in irregular circumstances, was something she could justify to herself.

But the idea of accepting hush-money for obliging this smiling, insincere woman—that was something quite different, and quite horrible!

She made her escape as soon as possible after that. And as she walked along Riverside Drive in the sunshine her mind was completely made up. Fate had played into her hands in an almost fantastic manner. Difficulties had been cleared away, whether she wanted it or not. She was to go to England.

CHAPTER THREE

'Less than an hour, Sonia, and then we should be in.'

Tina glanced up from the book which had been holding only half her attention in any case.

'Yes, we'll soon be home,' she agreed, smiling a little, because there was something so very pleasant about the way young Dr Morrison's eyes twinkled that one usually did want to smile in return.

It was a very alert twinkle, hardly in keeping with his slow, faintly drawling Southern voice. But then nor was his studiedly casual manner any indication of his keen and intensely living mind. Tina liked him all the more for that. There was something intriguing about such marked contrasts.

During the first hour or so out from New York, Tina had put him down as a charming but casual person, with no special aims or ideals. But in the enforced intimacy of the air cabin she had come to know him better. Earle Morrison had very definite aims and very definite ideals—though he might have hesitated to apply that word himself. His tone had been almost careless as he explained how he had given up a promising practice in order to come to England and give his services to a small and struggling research unit.

There was something rather reassuring about discussing other people's plans, Tina thought. It made one forget for a moment one's own fantastic and even perilous position.

'One of those ideas that come to you in the middle of the night, you know.' And he grinned. 'As a matter of fact, I've got a friend in England in a similar field. We were fellow students in Vienna several years ago. He's really what you mean by a swell guy.' He paused, in thoughtful contemplation of his remarkable friend, and Tina, knowing the American capacity for hero-worship, smiled sympathetically.

'He became a doctor too?' she inquired at last.

'Yes. Wizard of a fellow. We always kept up a fairly regular correspondence since the Vienna days.'

'So you have his own word for it that he's marvellous?' suggested Tina mischievously.

'His own—no, certainly not.'

'Oh, he's very modest about his achievements?'

'Well—no.' Earle Morrison grinned again in sudden real amusement. 'He knows he's a genius, come to that.'

'How horrid!'

'Not at all. You can't undo people's faces and put them together again unless you have a bit of self-confidence.'

'N—no,' Tina agreed. 'No, I should think it takes a good deal of courage. I wasn't really disparaging your friend's work. I only meant—one likes a man to wait and let others do the appreciating.'

'I don't think,' said Morrison reflectively, 'that Charles ever waited for anyone else to do something he thought he could do himself.'

'Even to blowing his own trumpet?'

'I'm sorry, I didn't mean to make him sound conceited. It's only that—oh, he has tremendous vitality and a great belief in himself, and he can be rather self-centred about it all, I suppose.'

'Well, I see he has the quality of making a very good friend, anyway.' And Tina smiled kindly, though she privately thought the casual, unassuming Earle Morrison was probably a great deal more likeable than the friend he admired so much.

After that there had been several talks between them— the sort of long, inconsequential talks that one has only while travelling, when the subjects range from food to religion and from chamber music to football. Sometimes Tina wished that the journey could go on for ever. She hated to remember that when it ended she would have to face what sometimes seemed a chain of unending risks and sometimes just the simple fulfilment of Sonia's wish and her own.

Even now, she could hardly believe that she had really taken on this extraordinary business. Each time anyone said 'Miss Frayne' she used to wonder if she gave the faintest start of surprise. But no one ever seemed to detect the slightest strangeness in her manner, and as hour succeeded hour on the rather monotonous trip, she had the curious impression that in leaving the New World for the Old, so she left the identity of her old self behind and gradually was transformed into Sonia Frayne. Not the Sonia Frayne she had known, of course, but a Sonia who was going home to England, to claim old Aunt Maggie's legacy.

It was odd how, at every turn, Fate had seemed to conspire to make the deception easy. Even after her conversation with Mrs Manton, and the oblique assurance that certainly no relation of Cyrus Manton would be anxious to give publicity to this third marriage, she had been afraid that some enterprising newspaperman would ferret out the romantic story that the millionaire had really been killed on a honeymoon trip. It was so exactly the sort of thing in which the newspapers delighted. But no mention was made of Sonia either by name or as 'a mystery girl'.

By some strange coincidence it seemed that the passenger list had never been completed, and the burnt-out wreck of the machine had provided tragically few clues as to the number and identities of the passengers. That 'three, if not four, other passengers, whose identity is as yet unknown' was the nearest they ever came to mentioning Sonia's presence.

Even the papers which Tina would need to help substantiate her claim seemed ready to her hand. Not only the passport itself, but letters from 'Aunt Maggie', and even— among several old and unimportant papers, kept for no special reason—a copy of Sonia's English birth certificate.

When Tina thought how securely her position was

buttressed, she told herself that it was ridiculous to feel even a flutter of nerves.

'And it isn't as though there's even anything fundamentally wrong about it,' she thought over and over again. 'Sonia wanted me to have the money—*meant* me to have the money. It was only a matter of days—perhaps hours—before the whole thing would have been made legal.'

Every detail went without a hitch. No one appeared to have dark suspicions about her identity. No one seemed to think she looked the dangerous kind of person who tried to enter on a false passport. And by the time she and Earle Morrison had found seats in the airport bus, her spirits were soaring and she was perfectly prepared to enjoy every moment of the journey.

She was home at last! Back in the only country that mattered to her. On every side she seemed to recognise dear, familiar sights, characteristic of the life she had remembered so poignantly and longed for so futilely until a few weeks ago.

'Well—happy to be back?'

She became aware that Earle was watching her with sympathetic amusement, and, flushing a little, she nodded.

'Oh, yes! You don't know how I've longed for this—summer and winter, waking and sleeping. It's the only country for me.'

'And yet you've been away from it most of your life, haven't you?'

The first bad slip! She must be more careful—*must* not get her facts muddled like this.

'Y-yes. But I've always dreamed of coming home,' she explained, and then hastily changed the subject.

It was a lovely journey after that. She had to pretend to find certain things as strange and unfamiliar as he did, but apart from that, there was no strain, because Earle was the easiest person in the world to be with.

Only when they were nearing London did he say something which profoundly disturbed her.

'I'm hoping Charles will meet us. I sent off a wire while I was waiting for you to get that trunk of yours cleared through the Customs. I hope he can make it—I'd like you to meet him. Maybe we could all have dinner together. That is'—he looked frankly inquiring—'if you haven't got people meeting you?'

'Oh, it's—very kind. But I'm sure you'll have lots to say to each other on your first evening. I don't think I'll turn it into a trio.' She thought she *must* find some way of cutting the threads which seemed to be entangling her pretty thoroughly.

'I'd like it tremendously if you'd come,' was the perfectly candid reply. 'And I know Charles would like you. He couldn't help it.'

Tina thought, in passing, that 'Charles' didn't sound the kind of person to take a hasty liking to anyone—and, equally, she felt perversely sure she would not like him. But anyway, that was not the really important point. The essential thing was that too many people should not know her as Sonia Frayne.

'I think I'll say "no", just the same,' she told Earle. 'It's sweet of you to ask me, but I'm really tired, and I think I'll make an early night of it.'

He was genuinely disappointed, she saw, but he said:

'Another time, then. I've got the name of your hotel, and I'll call you during the next few days.'

She agreed with a perfunctory smile, privately determining to move soon, leaving no address. At the moment, of course, it was impossible to make exact plans because she had next to no money of her own left. But she would go to see the lawyers first thing in the morning. And even if there were some delay about obtaining probate of 'Aunt Maggie's' will, no doubt they would advance her a reasonable sum. Then she could arrange just what she was going to do.

The bus was drawing into Central London now, and people were putting on coats and reaching for luggage.

Earle was already concerning himself with her cases, and evidently had no intention of leaving her until she was safely installed in a taxi.

He even seemed confident of being able to find her a porter amid the jostling throng of people at the air terminal.

'Here, you stand by this pillar for a moment'—he piled their luggage beside her—'and I'll go and find a porter.' And, worming his way between two family groups who were screaming rapturous greetings to each other, he disappeared in the crowd.

Tina didn't mind. She didn't mind being left. She didn't mind having to wait. She was home—back in London. She was home!

Suddenly she saw Earle slowly making his way back to her accompanied, not by a porter, but by a tall man in a light grey suit, who seemed to have as much to say to Earle as Earle had to say to him.

She would have recognised him at once from Earle's description. She thought she had never seen anything quite so arresting as that keen, slightly arrogant, laughing face. The very square jaw, the humorous mouth, the fine nose with unexpectedly sensitive nostrils, the extraordinarily brilliant blue eyes which narrowed now at the corners because Earle was saying something which evidently interested him enormously.

Tina was astonished that she could take in so much in the few seconds which she had before the two men came up with her. But she realised then, and ever afterwards, that the impression which Charles Linton made on people was instantaneous, clear-cut, and overwhelming.

He looked half startled when Earle stopped before her, as though he had been unwillingly recalled from something which really did interest him.

'I'm sorry—I haven't dug out that porter yet,' Earle explained with a laugh. 'But here's Charles. I ran into him almost at once. Charles, this is Miss Frayne—Sonia Frayne. We travelled together.'

'Good lord, how odd!' was Charles Linton's somewhat unexpected greeting.

'That we should have travelled together?' She looked amused.

'No. That your name should be Sonia Frayne. I think you must be some sort of cousin of mine.' And he regarded her with a cool interest which was not, she felt, particularly friendly.

It was as though someone had suddenly rung an alarm-bell which sounded high above all the other noises in the station, and for a moment Tiṇa could do nothing but repeat:

'Your—your cousin?'

'What an extraordinary thing!' That was Earle, sounding as though this was a discovery on which they might well be congratulated. 'But you didn't recognise Charles' name.'

'That's not surprising.' Those slightly narrowed eyes never left Tina's face. 'To tell the truth, I'd never heard of *her* until a month or two ago. But it seems you lived in dear Aunt Maggie's memory, my charming cousin.' And he made her an ironical little bow.

'Why—yes.' Tina spoke a trifle jerkily. 'Yes. Aunt Maggie has been very good to me.'

She thought it an extraordinary and rather dreadful coincidence that this man with the bright, penetrating eyes should even know about Aunt Maggie's legacy. He didn't *look* as though he were the kind of person to whom a thousand pound legacy would have much importance. And yet it was the first thing on which he commented.

She became aware that Earle was repeating his invitation to dinner that evening, sure that in the light of this new discovery she would reverse her decision.

'Come, Sonia, now it's a family affair, don't you think you might cancel that early night and come out with us? One doesn't meet a long-lost cousin every day. You ought to get to know each other.'

The long-lost cousin, she noticed, added nothing to this,

and she had the distinct impression that he had no special wish to 'get to know' her. Which was all to the good!

'No. No, really, thank you very much. You must excuse me.' Tina wondered if her tone sounded as agitated to Charles Linton as it did to her. 'I think the early start and the long journey are about all I can manage for today. A-another time, perhaps.'

'Another time most certainly.' Unexpectedly it was her so-called cousin, and not Earle Morrison, who got that in first. 'As your only relative in England—isn't that about right?—I feel bound to do the honours of your home country.'

'You needn't feel "bound" to do anything for me,' Tina assured him, with a sharpness which she immediately regretted.

He didn't attempt to conceal his amused surprise at her tone, and his quizzical smile made her blush furiously. He had, she noticed annoyedly, that gift, so much prized by those who possess it, of being able to raise one eyebrow without the other. He did it then, and she inevitably got the impression that he thought her a very odd little cousin, but one who might prove an amusing study.

That was the very last light in which she wished to appear to her by no means stupid new relation, and it was with a sensation of acute relief that she realised Earle had at last secured both a porter and a taxi.

Goodbyes were brief—though between her and Earle extremely cordial. Ordinarily he might have sought to prolong them, but evidently his thoughts were already running on to the long talk he was to have with his friend.

She could have wished he would not give the name of her hotel to the taxi-driver with quite such blithe distinctness, and she noticed uneasily that her cousin repeated it thoughtfully as though committing it to memory.

Somehow she maintained the rather strained smile on her face until the taxi drove away, and then she sank back on the worn and shiny seat with a sensation of genuine weakness. The shock of that sudden meeting combined with the necessity of keeping up appearances had been as much as she could bear.

Now she tried to assure herself that nothing really frightening had happened. It had always been conceivable that there would be one or two remote relations with whom she might have to have a casual meeting. If she met them no other way, she might very likely have had to see them at the lawyer's office. Was it any more alarming to have to meet one at the air terminal?

A pity he was quite such an alert and penetrating sort of person, of course. But he couldn't really be *very* much interested in her and her little legacy. If she took care not to see him again—or to see him only once—there was really not the least reason why he should feel any lively curiosity about her.

By the time Tina reached the quiet, rather old-fashioned hotel she had chosen, she had almost convinced herself that there was no reason for worry or alarm. She had already surmounted a large part of the difficulties and anxieties. It would be absurd to lose her nerve over a side-issue now. Far better concentrate on being calm and collected for her interview with the lawyers in the morning. That really would call for cool and steady nerves.

And yet, somehow, the thought of possibly meeting Charles Linton again disturbed her much more profoundly than the momentous interview with Aunt Maggie's lawyers.

She had determined to make an early call at the offices of Messrs. Medway & Medway, for since she had no appointment, she judged that her best chance of seeing whichever Mr Medway was concerned with her affairs would be to arrive before he started his appointments for the day.

The result was that she found a couple of typists in sole occupation of the offices of Messrs. Medway & Medway.

Fortunately for Tina, on the very stroke of ten-thirty the door of the outer office opened to admit a tall, grey-haired, severe-looking man, who passed through the room as Jove might have traversed the lower slopes of Olympus, ignoring both the secretaries and herself. Unquestionably this was Mr Medway.

A few minutes later she was ushered into the Presence.

She was aware that her breath was coming unusually quickly and that her legs felt curiously hollow, but she must have presented a perfectly normal appearance, she supposed, because Mr Medway greeted her with unexpected affability, a complete absence of suspicion, and a measured flow of conversation which was reassuring.

'Sit down, Miss Frayne, sit down. I am very pleased to make your acquaintance—and in such fortunate circumstances. I assume that you received my second letter?'

'A—second letter?' Tina felt acute anxiety in spite of his reassuring tone. 'I—didn't receive a second letter from you, Mr Medway. Only the one telling me about—about Aunt Maggie's death and that she had left me all she had.'

'Oh, I see, I see.' Mr Medway's affability took on an even richer tone, and every sign of severity had now melted. 'Then I have good news for you. Excellent news. In my first letter I think I gave you to understand that the late Miss Margaret Freeling's estate would not amount to more than a thousand pounds.'

He paused as though expecting confirmation of this, and Tina said nervously:

'Y-yes, that's right. You said you thought about—about a thousand.'

'A thousand,' agreed Mr Medway as though that insignificant sum now appeared to him scarcely worthy of mention in a letter. 'As the facts were known then, Miss Frayne, that sum was—roughly speaking—correct. Now, however, I am very glad to tell you, Miss Freeling died worth something in the region of—ah—let me see'—he put on a pair of spectacles and consulted some papers—'yes—sixty thousand pounds.'

'Sixty *thousand*! It's impossible!' Tina actually rose to her feet, in something that was more dismay than delight.

Mr Medway appeared to recognise the reaction for what

it was. Looking over his spectacles he observed soothingly:

'Very sudden, of course. But surely rather a—rather an enjoyable shock, Miss Frayne, than otherwise?'

Tina sat down slowly again.

'Y-yes,' she stammered. 'Yes, of course. Only it's such an enormous sum.' She meant—such an enormous sum to come by not quite honestly! 'One feels that—someone else ought to benefit too.'

Mr Medway didn't seem to feel that at all. He looked at Tina in surprise and said, somewhat sententiously:

'The sentiment does your heart credit, Miss Frayne, but there is really no need for you to take that view.'

Tina smiled faintly.

'I meant—it seems that almost anyone else must have known Aunt Maggie better than I did. She only knew me as a baby. I—I can't remember her at all.' Tina suddenly realised she was unconsciously doing this rather well. 'I feel as though *someone* must surely resent an unknown niece coming back after years and—and getting everything.'

'Such a view would be absolutely unjustified and most improper,' Mr Medway assured her firmly. 'The terms of your aunt's will were clear and explicit. We drew up the will for her some years ago,' he added, as though that finally disposed of any objection.

'Oh, I didn't mean that legally there was any doubt. Only that—that——'

'Yes, I see what you mean,' Mr Medway conceded graciously. 'You feel that someone else might conceivably have expected to benefit, and experience some disappointment now.'

'Y-yes.' Tina supposed that described it as well as anything. 'Was there anyone who—who might have felt like that?' she asked, as though unable to stop herself.

'No one,' asserted Mr Medway firmly, 'except perhaps your cousin, Charles Linton.'

CHAPTER FOUR

TINA stared at Mr Medway for a few seconds in silence. Then with rather dry lips she repeated:

'Charles Linton?'

'Of course, I make no suggestion that he does entertain any such feelings,' Mr Medway hastened to add. 'I was only answering your—ah—objection by pointing out that he was absolutely the only person who *could* conceivably have such a feeling.'

'Yes—I see. Tell me'—Tina was frowning slightly—'what was his relationship with Aunt Maggie? I mean, were they very friendly? Had he any reason to think she would leave him anything.'

'We-ell'—Mr Medway appeared to give the matter his earnest attention—'to the best of my belief they were on quite friendly, though hardly intimate, terms, and as of course none of us anticipated that your Aunt Margaret would ever have any great sum of money to leave, there was no reason why Mr Linton should be greatly interested in the matter one way or another. I imagine he does quite well in his profession. He would hardly be much exercised in his mind as to whether or not he would inherit a few hundred from his aunt.'

'And how is it that there is suddenly this—this extraordinary sum involved?'

'Ah, now, that is really a very interesting story!' And Mr Medway, with whom family histories were evidently a matter of passionate interest, settled down to tell this one with gusto. 'As you probably know, the late Miss Margaret Freeling was one of three sisters. Your mother, though

42

adopted into the family and regarded always as a fourth sister, was really no blood relation at all.'

'No, I know that,' murmured Tina, with a glib untruthfulness that surprised and half dismayed her.

'Quite evidently, however, Miss Margaret regarded your mother as a favourite sister, and her interest in you was doubtless the result of this. Of the other two sisters, Miss Beatrice married and had one son—your cousin, Charles Linton. Though, of course,' added Mr Medway, with earnest accuracy, 'he is not really your cousin. The other sister also married and went to South Africa. I believe she kept up a desultory correspondence with Miss Margaret, but she never returned to England. Her husband appears to have made a considerable fortune, and predeceased her. She herself died a few months ago, and having no family of her own, left everything to your Aunt Margaret.'

'And poor old Aunt Maggie never lived to enjoy it!' exclaimed Tina with genuine regret. It seemed hard that the old lady who had been, unwittingly, so generous to her should have missed a comfortable fortune by a few weeks.

'She never lived to enjoy it,' Mr Medway agreed. 'But,' he added, intent on the legal aspect of the matter, 'there is no question but that her sister predeceased her. In other words, Miss Margaret *had* inherited her sister's fortune before her own death, and as she left you everything of which she died possessed, you, Miss Frayne, are unquestionably the heiress to the whole amount.'

Tina nodded slowly, wishing she didn't feel the most unutterable fraud. To accept a thousand pounds—intended for her anyway—in rather doubtful circumstances was one thing. It was quite another to accept sixty thousand!

But how could one make a graceful retreat at this point?

It was impossible simply to disappear, leaving matters to settle themselves. Mr Medway was, she could see, the kind of man to pursue things to the bitter end. He was quite capable of setting on foot all sorts of inquiries and investigations in order to trace what—Tina realised with a shudder—would then have become 'the missing heiress'.

And she, of all people, could not afford to have her affairs investigated too closely.

There was no way out of it. She was, as one might say, compelled to accept sixty thousand pounds, whether she liked it or not!

It hardly surprised her, after that, to find that the rest of the interview went with velvety smoothness. She seemed absolutely fated to receive that money, and nothing in her claim, or the documents supporting it, appeared to awake the slightest doubts in Mr Medway's thoughts.

He asked her very courteously to leave the papers with him for examination, but his own acceptance of their authenticity was shown by the fact that when she explained the difficulty of having had to arrive in the country with practically no money, he unhesitatingly advanced her a sum of two hundred pounds out of her 'aunt's' estate.

And Tina didn't think Mr Medway was at all the man to pay out money which he did not confidently expect to see back again!

If anyone had told her an hour ago that she would leave Mr Medway's office with two hundred pounds and a feeling of great uneasiness, she would have thought the idea ridiculous. But that was exactly what she did.

Rather slowly and very thoughtfully Tina made her way along Fleet Street and the Strand, so intent on her present problem that she hardly appreciated the wonderful fact that she was back in dear and familiar surroundings. Crossing the top of Northumberland Avenue and Whitehall, she made her way into the Park, and having found a seat where the alternate sun and shadow made a pleasant pattern, she sat down to consider her present position.

It would be ridiculous to pretend, even to oneself, that sixty thousand pounds, as such, were unwelcome. Tina made no such pretence. Only she ardently wished that the sum could have come to her unaccompanied by these terrible qualms of conscience.

Might one assume that Sonia—if she could have expressed a wish—would have wanted her friend to inherit all that money?—so much, much more than the already generous gift of a thousand pounds.

But then Sonia had *not* expressed any wish, and was certainly not the kind of girl ever to make a will, even if she had had time to do so. In no conceivable circumstances could those sixty thousand pounds have been legally left to Tina. The fortune had come her way simply by chance and —one must face the fact—by something like fraud.

Tina winced as she came to that final conclusion. She *was* defrauding someone. Not to put too fine a point on it, she was defrauding her so-called cousin, Charles Linton. For since Sonia had died without leaving a will, Charles, as the sole surviving relation of the family, should surely inherit everything. At least, so far as Tina's somewhat sketchy legal knowledge went, that seemed the right and proper conclusion.

No wonder he had looked at her yesterday evening with a curiosity not entirely friendly. Evidently he was personally known to Mr Medway, and he would naturally have been told of the large legacy which had come into, and—if the truth be told—also left, the family with such unusual suddenness.

'If he knew the real facts,' thought Tina uncomfortably, 'there would be a good deal more than that cool reserve in his manner.'

A few hours ago her one idea had been that she never wanted to see Charles Linton again. Now she had an uneasy desire to study him again, in the light of the new discovery. If only he had been an easy and understanding person, one might almost—well, not have told him the true facts, of course—but come to some sort of arrangement, suggested that it was hardly right that she, an absolute stranger, should inherit everything.

Tina bit her lip at this point. Charles Linton had not seemed at all the kind of person with whom one could make an unorthodox arrangement like that. He would want to know the whys and wherefores, and she hardly thought she would relish the task of pulling wool over those shrewd, bright eyes.

And yet one must do something! At least, if one were ever to have a quiet conscience again.

Tina had not come to any sort of decision, even by the time she returned to her hotel for lunch. The clerk at the desk glanced at her as she came in, and handed her a note which read:

'Dr Earle Morrison telephoned. Ringing later.'

Certainly Earle was not losing any time. She had hardly finished her lunch before she was called to the telephone.

'Hello there! Aren't you an elusive sort of person?'

Earle's friendly, drawling voice made her smile. It was nice to feel there was someone in London who knew and liked her.

'Why? Did you ring more than once?' she wanted to know.

'No. But I called you early, and they said you'd already gone out.'

'Oh yes, I had to go—somewhere on business.'

'I see. How about dinner tonight? Could you make it?'

There was a moment's hesitation. Somehow today it didn't seem anything like so necessary to avoid Earle as it had yesterday. And anyway, one could hardly go on re-fusing his invitations without creating a rather peculiar impression.

'Yes, I'd love it. When and where?'

'Say seven-thirty, here. At the Bosanquet.'

Tina agreed, and only when she had rung off, did she wonder if he intended this to be a tête-à-tête dinner, as originally arranged, or whether he intended to make it simply the postponed meal which he had suggested they should share with her new-found relation.

In her present state of mind she was not quite sure which she wanted it to be, for struggling with her nervous dread of meeting Charles Linton again, was a sort of fascinated interest in him—partly because of his overwhelming personality and partly because of the place he now held in her own affairs.

As Tina dressed for her appointment that evening, she was distinctly aware of a desire to look her best. Because Earle was so nice, she supposed.

The Bosanquet was a considerably larger and more fashionable hotel than the one at which she herself was staying, but she guessed that it would probably not be necessary to wear evening dress. So she put on one of the few really good dresses she possessed—a fine black wool, cut on severe lines.

Sonia had once said that there was a certain sophisticated innocence about that dress. And remembering that now with a smile, Tina decided that the innocence would do for Earle and the sophistication for—anyone else who happened to see her.

Slipping on a cream wool coat, which had already given her good service but always looked well, she surveyed the final effect in the mirror.

Yes, she looked her best. Not bright and polished and utterly sophisticated like Sonia, of course, but—the black emphasised the delicate tones of her complexion and gave a soft brilliance to the very fair hair which curled almost in a fringe over her forehead and was worn long behind.

As she entered the foyer of the hotel her first thought was, 'What a crowd! Shall I ever be able to find Earle?'

Then the throng seemed to break up into its component parts, grouping in couples and larger parties, and only a few individuals—standing by pillars or near the wall —waited for their companions.

She stood for a moment herself, glancing at each single figure in turn. Then someone came up and said, 'Good evening, Miss Frayne.' And it was not Earle. It was Charles Linton.

'Oh——' She hesitated, and then instinctively took the hand held out to her. 'Good evening. I—wasn't sure whether you were coming or not.'

'Earle was good enough to invite me too,' he assured her, those slightly amused bright eyes watching her as he spoke. 'As a matter of fact he's just telephoned to say that he was out of London this afternoon and has been delayed coming back. He hopes to join us in about half an hour, but he asked me to meet you and make his excuses.'

'Oh, I—see.' She was nonplussed for the first moment, and then curiously excited.

'If you're hungry, we have Earle's permission to start dinner without him, or——'

'Oh, I think we'll wait for him, don't you?'

'Yes, I think so too. Shall we go into the lounge and have a drink and—get to know each other?'

She laughed, a little nervously.

'That seems a good idea. It's—funny that we're really related, and yet haven't met each other until yesterday, isn't it?'

'I suppose that was inevitable, considering the Atlantic Ocean was between us.'

'But you were over in the States once, weren't you?'

'For quite a short visit. And you? You haven't been back to England since you were an infant, I believe?'

'No,' Tina said, hating the lie. 'No, I haven't.'

There didn't seem much else to say until they were comfortably settled in a quiet corner of the lounge and drinks had been placed before them. Then, with a sort of desperate rashness, she plunged straight into the most thorny subject.

'I—went to see Mr Medway this morning.'

'Oh—yes?' He was polite, but not overwhelmingly interested, it seemed.

'He—told me about—about Aunt Maggie's big legacy.'

'Yes, of course. You didn't know about it until this morning?'

'No. At least, I had no idea of the size of it. When he wrote to—to me first, he thought it was only about a thousand pounds.'

'I see. And since then Aunt Carrie's little lot rolled in?'

'Y-yes.'

'You must be feeling pretty well on top of the world at the moment, then.' He didn't look at her, but smiled that rather disturbing little smile, and thoughtfully studied his whisky.

'Well—yes. I mean—no.'

'No?' He glanced up quickly, and for the twentieth time she was struck by the extraordinary penetration of his look. 'What's the snag?'

'Don't you think I might very well feel extremely uncomfortable about the whole business?' she said slowly.

'No.' He was dryly positive about that. 'It must take an extraordinarily sensitive nature to feel uncomfortable about receiving sixty thousand pounds.'

'In the circumstances?'

'What circumstances, my little cousin?' he said quietly.

She flushed when he called her that—at least half with pleasure, she realised in some surprise.

'Charles—may I call you that?'

'It seems the most reasonable thing, Sonia,' he agreed gravely.

'I can't help feeling that you ought to have had at least some of that money.'

'I can't help feeling the same,' he said with a cool smile. 'But our feeling happens to be wrong, you know.'

'No, it doesn't! Aunt—what was her name?—Carrie— you see I couldn't even remember her name for the moment!—Aunt Carrie could never have intended *me* to have her money. She probably hardly knew that I existed, and anyway, I'm no real relation. Mother—Mother wasn't even their sister, you know.'

'I know. But then, you see, she left the money to Aunt Maggie and Aunt Maggie was perfectly entitled to leave it to you. Q.E.D.'

'Ethically it's all wrong.' Tina found she was quite hot about the argument by now.

'But legally quite right.' She saw he was a good deal amused at her earnestness.

'Must one consider only the legal aspect?'

'Why, of course. What else did you want to consider?'

'Well, what I said—the ethical side of it.'

He shook his head thoughtfully, but still smiled in a way that made her feel he was not very serious about the business.

'I'm afraid however much my natural cupidity and your natural—delicacy enter into it, the ethics are quite sound too.'

'Charles'—she couldn't smile, if he could—'won't you let us come to some—arrangement about it?'

'No, you funny child, I won't,' he said with a laugh.

'I'm not that!'

'What?'

'A funny child.'

'No?' He studied her judicially. 'You're an unworldly little thing, anyway. A strange product for New York. What on earth did you do there—for a living, I mean?'

'I—played the violin in a nightclub.'

'Good God!'

'Yes, it was rather frightful sometimes.'

'No, I meant—it's the last thing on earth I could have imagined you doing. It's all wrong for your type. So is your name, of course,' he added thoughtfully.

'My—my name?'

'Yes. You don't look in the least a Sonia.'

'Why not?' She passed the tip of her tongue over lips that had grown suddenly dry.

'We-ell, don't you think "Sonia" sounds bright and sophisticated and just a little hard?'

She couldn't answer him. She could only stare in a sort of superstitious dread. It was as though he had raised Sonia's very ghost.

'Don't look like that.' He laughed, rather puzzledly, and put his hand over hers not unkindly.

She glanced down at the hand. It was long and strong and brown. An extraordinarily fine hand, with undoubted strength in it.

'Well?' he said as she remained silent.

'N-nothing.' She glanced up, stammering a little with the confusion of her thoughts. 'I—was thinking what—what nice hands you have.'

'Really?' He was quite unabashed, and regarded his hands with the same critical amusement he was inclined to direct on her. 'Oh, they're all right. At least they are useful hands.'

'In your work, you mean?' She looked at him with half-shy curiosity. 'You're—very fond of your work, aren't you?'

'Very,' he agreed briefly.

'I can't connect you with it, somehow. It seems—frivolous for you.'

'Frivolous!' He looked astounded. 'That's the first time I've ever heard surgery described as frivolous.'

'Oh, but—it isn't surgery in the usual sense, is it? I think Earle said you specialised in plastic surgery.'

'Well?' His surprise remained for a moment. Then suddenly he gave a scornful laugh. 'Oh, you goose! I suppose that suggests lifting dowagers' faces and disguising gangsters, to your mind?'

'I'm sorry.' She flushed. 'Have I been rather a fool?'

'Very much so,' he assured her coolly.

'Then it's something very different?'

'Yes, Sonia. Something very different. It is remaking shattered faces and bodies and—sometimes shattered lives.'

'Oh!' In that moment she sensed something of his passionate obsession with his work. 'How—thrilling, Charles.'

'Yes,' he said slowly. 'It's thrilling. To see your work in terms of re-made lives—it's thrilling. That's why——' He stopped and laughed suddenly, and to her surprise she saw that he had flushed slightly in his turn.

'Yes? That's why——?'

'Nothing.' He frowned and shook his head. 'Something quite personal, and decidedly tactless.'

'I don't think that really worries you,' Tina said calmly. 'Suppose you tell me.'

He shrugged, and the momentary embarrassment disappeared so completely that she wondered if it had ever really been there.

'Very well, then. That is why I presumed to think the money from our late lamented aunts could have run very usefully through *my* hands.'

'Yes, I agree with you,' Tina said soberly. 'Then *now* will you let us—let us come to some sort of arrangement?'

'In spite of the beautifully tactful way of putting it, I will not,' he assured her, just a trifle mockingly.

'But why *not*?' She felt almost that he enjoyed the discomfort which her legacy caused her. If he had known!

'Why not? Because one can't cast a covetous eye on a large sum of money belonging to someone else and just think, "I could use that. If it's offered, I shall take it."'

'You know it isn't like that.'

'Near enough.'

'Charles, I think you're disgustingly exasperating!'

'Do you?' He was quite cool about it. 'Cousins usually are, I believe.'

'Meaning that you think I am?'

'Well—persistent with the charitable offers, shall we say.'

'I'm sorry, I didn't mean to—hurt or offend you.'

'It takes much more than that to offend me,' he assured her with a brilliant smile. 'And ten times more than that to hurt me.'

She thought it must be nice to be so gloriously self-sufficient, and armed against outside influences.

'Then you don't put me down as exasperating?'

He considered her amusedly again and said:

'No. But shockingly unworldly. Don't go about offering your fortune so eagerly to any other deserving cases. You may come up against someone who hasn't got my beautiful and disinterested disposition. Then you'll be skinned of everything, and I shall have a penniless and bewildered cousin to add to my other cares.'

'Do you really suppose I should come to you if I were in trouble?' she inquired indignantly, extremely nettled by his smiling confidence.

'No.' He regarded her negligently. 'I should probably have to find it out for myself.'

'How dare you!' She gave an angry little laugh.

'How dare I what?'

'Suggest that I—that I am any responsibility of yours.'

He leant his arms on the small table between them and smiled full at her.

'And aren't you?'

'Why, of course not!' In one sense she was horrified at the idea—it implied a dangerous degree of interest in her movements—and in another she was angrily intrigued that he should advance such a preposterous theory with such smiling calm.

It was difficult to say whether he would have maintained the claim or just let the subject go, for at that moment Earle arrived—apologetic and rather transparently anxious to know how they had got on together. Perhaps he had sensed the faint antagonism at the air terminal the previous day. For all his casual air, he was sensitive to atmosphere, and the glance which he gave now from his friend to Tina was a little quizzical.

But if he had expected to find an increase of tension, he was mistaken. As they accompanied him into the grill-room, they appeared admirably in accord, and during the meal conversation flowed easily and pleasantly.

More than once during that evening Tina asked herself anxiously if hers were really a nature that took quite naturally to deception. 'Certainly I'm doing this very well,' she reflected grimly.

In spite of any secret anxiety, she found she was able to smile and talk with Earle—even to meet Charles' glance calmly and with every appearance of confidence. And all the time she was thinking:

'Have I really settled the question of this legacy? Can I possibly leave things as they are? I've done my very best to make him listen to reason. What else *can* I do? I dare not go on arguing the matter indefinitely. He's no fool. He'll begin to suspect something.'

And yet she knew that if she did leave things as they were, her conscience would torment her endlessly.

That money belonged to Charles, by every right—legal or moral. Somehow, somehow, she must see that he got it. The simple question was—how?

For one moment, and one moment only, she toyed with the idea of telling him the real truth. Then a single glance at that uncompromising profile made her shrink from the idea with horror. For a man who smiled easily, he could give an extraordinarily forbidding impression. Tina didn't think she would like to be the person who owned to having cheated and fooled him.

Curiously enough, the two men were speaking just then of someone they both knew and apparently had reason to dislike. Earle said: 'He just doesn't know the difference between right and wrong. That's all there is to it.'

And Charles, with a rather frightening gleam in his eye, said dryly:

'My dear fellow, you flatter him. He *does* know the difference between right and wrong, but it doesn't happen to interest him.'

Tina glanced from one to the other with such an expression of serious concentration that Earle laughed suddenly and remarked:

'We're boring Sonia with talk of someone she doesn't know.'

'Oh no,' Tina assured him, 'I wasn't bored. I was interested.'

'In what?' Charles wanted to know.

'In your different reactions to someone you both disapprove of, I suppose.'

'*Are* our reactions different?' Earle smiled questioningly.

'Oh—very. You're rather tolerant, I think, even about people you—you catch out.'

'And I——?' inquired her cousin quietly.

Tina looked at him, more sadly than she knew.

'I shouldn't like to have to depend on your tolerance,' she said slowly.

Whereat he laughed and said, 'Quite right, my little cousin,' in that cool, positive way of his.

'It's no good,' thought Tina, in a sort of desperation. 'I can't do anything else about it. It may be cowardly. It may be dishonest. I've *got* to go on with things now. Even if I wrote a letter of explanation and disappeared, *someone* would find it their duty to track me down for having entered the country on a false passport. That's what catches me every time! What a fool I was ever to do this!'

And yet she knew that, if she could find herself back in the Brooklyn apartment, with the necessity of going on night after night at the club, subject to the whims and temper of Louis, chained to work she hated in an atmosphere she loathed—she would probably stifle the voice of her conscience and take almost any way of escape. It had been just bearable until she glimpsed freedom. Now she would literally rather die than give up even this doubtful security in the country she loved.

She would have to stiffen her resolution and go on somehow. Above all, there must be no more intimate talks with her so-called cousin. It shouldn't be difficult to avoid him. A busy doctor, without the slightest interest in her existence until a few weeks ago—why *should* he want to see much of her?

By the time the party broke up she was thinking:

'It's been lovely, but it mustn't happen again. The less I see of both of them, the better. Perhaps I can go out of London for a while, and by the time I come back, they'll have other interests. No more talks alone with Charles——'

And at that moment he said:

'I'll see my cousin to her hotel, Earle. It's on my way.'

'Sure?'

'Yes. Quite sure.'

There was nothing she could do about it—except say goodnight to Earle and go with her cousin.

As they came out of the hotel, the warm summer air greeted them.

'Oh, isn't it lovely!' Tina breathed involuntarily. And her cousin paused, smiling a little. Then, as though another thought had struck him, he said:

'Would you prefer to walk?'

'Is it safe?'

'Safe? Oh yes.' He laughed softly. 'This isn't New York, you know. Besides—in spite of the rebuff this evening—I undertake to take care of you.'

And, taking her hand, he drew it through his arm, holding it lightly against his side in a warm, personal contact which suddenly set her heart beating inexplicably fast.

CHAPTER FIVE

AFTERWARDS Tina used to look back on that short walk to her hotel as something very significant in her relationship with Charles Linton.

It was not that her instinctive antagonism to him entirely disappeared, but it somehow became merged in her fascinated interest in him. An interest which—she realised it now—had more to do with him as an individual than the fact that she had become forcibly related to him and very much entangled in his private affairs.

He, for his part, appeared to have little more than this casual, half-amused interest in her, and Tina shrewdly suspected that there were few things besides his work to which he did pay the tribute of any more serious attention.

Even when he asked her about her future plans—which he did as they walked through the almost deserted streets —he did so more as though it were a question one might be expected to ask than a matter in which he had any specially lively interest.

'I don't know that I've made any definite plans yet,' Tina said slowly, very sure that at any rate she could not discuss them in detail with him.

'Well, you'll be able to afford to live where you like— even in the gilded security of the stockbroker belt,' he remarked carelessly.

'But I don't want gilded security,' Tina assured him quickly. 'I didn't come home to be a—a parasite.'

'No?' He sounded amused—not very politely so. 'But then you didn't know you were coming home to sixty thousand pounds, remember.'

'Well, do you suppose that inheriting money necessarily changes one's character?'

'Never having inherited any, I'm afraid I can't say.'

She was silent at that. And then after a few moments she spoke slowly and thoughtfully.

'If *you* had inherited Aunt Maggie's money, what would you have done?'

'You sound like a reporter interviewing a sweepstake winner,' he told her lightly. 'And I believe the classic reply is—I should just go on with my work.'

'Yes, I know that bit!' She laughed, though a little vexedly that he so determinedly refused to take her seriously. 'But haven't you any idea of what you would do with a suddenly acquired fortune? Most people have.'

'Have they?' And then, after a moment, with real curiosity, 'Had you?'

'Yes, of course. I meant to come home to England.'

'Just that? Nothing else?'

'It seemed enough, all those dreadful four years,' Tina murmured, half to herself.

'What four years?' He sounded puzzled, and she felt her teeth knock together with the terrified realisation of what she had said.

'Oh, I meant the—the last four years. In New York, you know. I wasn't always there. But—but that was the worst time.' She hoped that didn't sound as jerky to him as it did to her. Apparently not, because he just said reflectively:

'Was it? Funny. I liked New York—every moment of it.'

'But then,' Tina pointed out, without rancour, 'you were not playing in a third-rate nightclub.'

He laughed.

'That's true.' Then, after a pause, 'So the one thing you meant to do if money came your way was to come back to the country you left as a baby?'

'Yes.' She spoke rather breathlessly. 'And—and what did you mean to do? You haven't told me yet.'

'Well,' he said slowly, 'I suppose until fairly recently I should have used any unexpected windfall to help to establish a special clinic for my particular kind of surgery. Something like that. Something where I could afford to disregard the financial side of things altogether and simply concentrate on research—special cases—fresh developments, and that sort of thing.'

She had no time to question him further as the shape of her hotel loomed before them. Charles stayed with her no longer than to see she was safely inside the entrance to the hotel. Then he left her with an abruptness which suggested that he had much more important things on hand than the affairs of a remote relation.

That was as it should be, for no doubt he *had* more important things to do. But as Tina made her way to her room she found her thoughts irresistibly following Charles, before, tired by by the events of the day, she fell asleep.

It was the next morning—free, for the first time, from any immediate tasks or worries—that Tina began to realise that a life of deception was perforce also a life of considerable isolation.

Common sense demanded that she should make as few acquaintances as possible until her position was clearer and her plans more definite. For each person who came to know her as 'Miss Frayne' added to the complications of her future. Indeed, an uneasy conviction was growing upon her that if the circle were extended much further, she would find herself trapped into remaining Miss Frayne to the end of her days.

But, in spite of these clear-sighted reflections, Tina was acutely conscious of an illogical desire to be sociable—to chat with someone, preferably with some other girl. Not about anything in particular—just an exchange of views on everyday things. One couldn't exist on momentous interviews with lawyers, nerve-racking conversations with dangerous cousins, or even casual comments from mistaken, elderly waiters.

'I'd just like to talk for the sake of talking,' thought Tina. 'If only Sonia——'

She broke off with that slight sense of shock which the memory of Sonia still brought. So difficult to remember that there *was* no Sonia now. No real Sonia. Only herself in some masquerade which even now sometimes seemed too strange to be true.

She shivered, because these recollections were depressing, and—caution forgotten—she turned with real relief as someone came over and dropped comfortably into the opposite corner of the lounge settee, evidently with the intention of addressing her.

As Tina glanced up she met the smiling, frankly curious gaze of very bright dark eyes, and she reflected absently—though with real admiration—that the girl who was watching her had remarkably pretty teeth. Otherwise she was not outstandingly good-looking, but she had a certain youthful air of extreme interest which arrested attention and imparted an unmistakable friendliness to her manner.

'Hello!' the girl said, without any preamble. 'Have coffee with me, will you? I'm tired of my own company and I'm hoping you are of yours.'

Tina smiled. It was impossible not to, in the face of such engaging frankness.

'Thank you, I'd like coffee. And—yes, I'd like to talk too.' Too late to remember that it would have been wiser to plead an urgent engagement. And the girl was ordering coffee and arranging the cushions into a more comfortable position behind her head before Tina could modify her admission.

'My name's Audrey Unsworth,' she informed Tina, still with that complete lack of ceremony, 'and we've been turned out of our flat, and I'm simply furious with everyone, because I don't like living in this place. Do you?'

'I've been here only a couple of days,' Tina explained with a smile, 'and it seems comfortable enough. It will do until—until I get a place of my own.'

'Oh, well, that's different, of course. It's the reverse

process that's so infuriating. Coming here *from* a place of one's own.'

'I'm—sorry about your having to leave your flat,' Tina murmured with what she hoped was an air of tactful sympathy. From her companion's slightly dramatic way of imparting the information she rather wondered whether bailiffs had had something to do with the hasty exit. It was difficult to inquire—but it also proved unnecessary, for Miss Unsworth appeared to suffer from no special reticence about her private affairs.

'The landlord came back in a hurry and more or less turfed us out as our lease was up.'

'I suppose he needed it,' Tina suggested mildly.

'I didn't believe a word he said. But there you are. Life's like that, isn't it?'

Tina agreed cautiously that, broadly speaking, life was often like that.

'Anyway, it's a good thing it didn't happen until after Eileen had gone.'

Tina waited while coffee was poured out, in the hope that Eileen's identity would be made a little clearer. It was, almost immediately.

'Eileen's my sister,' her companion explained. 'She lived with me in the flat. Now she's gone to take up nursing.'

'Oh yes?' Tina felt that some comment was called for, but that the only kind of comment which would be appreciated would be an invitation to continue the monologue. 'How interesting!' She hoped that sounded convincing.

'Oh, do you think so? I don't a bit. I'd much rather be a model or test pilot.'

'Yes,' Tina agreed, wondering for the first time how old the adventurous Miss Unsworth was. Under twenty probably, judging from her views. 'But your sister voted for nursing?'

'Um-hm. Not that Eileen had the usual illusions about it, of course.'

'The usual illusions?'

'Yes. You know how lots of girls think it's all pillow-smoothing and smiling at good-looking doctors. And all the time it's really mostly bed-pans and being nagged by the Matron.'

Tina laughed.

'But that didn't discourage your sister?'

'N-no.' For the first time Audrey Unsworth hesitated in her rapid flow of conversation. Then, with apparent irrelevance, she volunteered the information:

'I saw you coming in yesterday evening. That was the first time I noticed you.'

'Was it?'

'Yes. I was in the entrance hall. That was Mr Linton with you, wasn't it? Charles Linton, the surgeon.'

'Why, yes!' Tina spoke a little more sharply than she had intended, and she could not help glancing quickly at her questioner. 'Do you know him, then?'

'Oh no. At least, not to speak to. But that was one reason why I thought I'd like to get to know you. You see, *he's* one reason why Eileen wanted to do nursing.'

Tina thought the reasoning was becoming slightly mixed, and frowned in a puzzled way.

'I'm afraid I don't quite see,' she confessed. 'Why exactly did Eileen take up nursing?—and what had it to do with Charles—Mr Linton?'

'Goodness! Do you know him well enough to call him by his first name?' Her hearer was embarrassingly impressed.

'He's a sort of cousin,' Tina explained, biting her lip, because she was a little vexed at being trapped into admitting as much. 'But do tell me about Eileen.'

'Oh, well, you see, she'd done first aid work and all that sort of thing, and suddenly she got a chance of pulling a string or two and getting taken on at Charles Linton's hospital. At least, I mean the hospital where he does most of his work.'

'Does she admire his work so much or something?'

The younger Miss Unsworth gave a scornful sound indicative of extreme amusement.

'You could put it that way, I suppose,' was what she said.

Tina smiled.

'Or how else could one put it?' she asked.

'We-ell—I don't really know why I'm being so frank to you.' A belated discretion seemed to descend upon Miss Unsworth. 'Eileen's always saying that I talk far too much.'

Tina privately thought Eileen was probably painfully correct, and she said at once:

'Well, don't tell me anything of your sister's private affairs. I only thought——'

'Oh, that's all right. *I* started it.' Audrey Unsworth admitted generously. Then, after another of those pauses during which she studied Tina with an attention that would have been embarrassing if it had not been so ingenuous: 'Would you mind if I asked you something frightfully personal?'

'I don't expect so.' Tina was amused again.

'I mean—*really* something that isn't my business at all.'

'Well, I could refuse to answer if I didn't like the question,' Tina pointed out mildly.

'Yes—of course, you could. I only wondered—you're not engaged or anything to Charles Linton, are you?'

'Certainly not,' replied Tina, with a promptness that seemed to dispose of the vague 'or anything' quite as finally as with the suggestion of an engagement.

'Good!' Her hearer drew an unmistakable sigh of relief.

'Why?' Tina could not resist asking—her curiosity getting the better of her.

'Well, I *think* Eileen means to marry him. And it's always so much nicer for everyone around if Eileen gets just what she wants,' was the rather astonishing reply.

Tina tried—without success—to imagine what Charles' reactions would be to these matrimonial efforts on his behalf. Aloud she said:

'But does your sister know him very well?'

'Not very,' Audrey Unsworth admitted with characteristic candour. 'But you simply can't imagine what a determined person Eileen is when she wants anything. She's much more worldly and sophisticated and all that sort of thing than I am, and she always knows just exactly what she wants.'

Tina couldn't help wondering if Eileen's ideas on marriage were to be taken about as seriously as her sister's ideas on careers. But the next sentence disposed of that.

'Eileen's lots older than I am, you know. Nearly thirty —though she'd be furious if she knew I said so.'

'I see. Reached an age of discretion and knows her own mind.' Tina smiled, though for some reason or other she felt disquieted as well as amused by the conversation. 'So she's very fond of my charming cousin?'

Miss Unsworth wrinkled her nose sceptically.

'Funny how you keep on using all the wrong words to describe Eileen,' she said. 'I shouldn't say she was *fond* of anyone. Except herself, of course,' she added, with a singular lack of rancour for an unloved younger sister. 'You see, she always meant to marry someone—someone with their foot on the ladder of fame, as you might say.'

'Really?' Tina felt her eyebrows go up almost without her own volition. 'And does that describe Mr Linton?'

'Oh, rather. "Brilliant surgeon of the younger generation —specialising in plastic surgery." I mean—the headlines positively write themselves.'

Tina laughed rather vexedly, and her companion exclaimed with sudden anxiety:

'I say, you won't feel it your duty to warn him or anything, will you?'

'No,' Tina said, a trifle dryly. 'I imagine Charles Linton is very well able to look after himself without any cousinly warnings.'

'Very likely. Though, of course,' murmured Audrey reflectively, 'you don't know Eileen.'

Tina couldn't help feeling that she had no wish to know

Eileen either. The whole episode was becoming rather silly and irritating, and anyway, one could hardly be expected to take it seriously.

Still rather dryly she said:

'Is Eileen so extremely attractive? Or on what does she base her rather—rather exaggerated hopes?'

'Oh, didn't I explain that?' Audrey flickered her lashes with an ingenuousness which Tina felt to be almost—though not quite—too good to be true. 'She's quite attractive, of course. But the real point is that she has money. We both have—only mine's tied up until I'm twenty-one.'

Tina wondered with some embarrassment how many more intimate facts about the Unsworth family were to be presented to her, free, gratis, and for nothing, and rather hastily she said:

'And does Eileen expect money to have an irresistible appeal to her vic—I mean——'

'That's all right, you can call him a victim, if you like. I know what you mean. And yes, she does. After all, he stated quite frankly that he intended to marry money.'

'He what?' Tina was really startled into interest at last. 'When did he make this—this frank statement, pray?'

'Oh, you needn't be stiff about it,' her companion assured her cheerfully. 'Lots of ambitious men intend to marry money, only very few of them are honest enough to admit it. He said it at some party Eileen was at—quite a small party. I suppose they were discussing marriage more or less seriously, and someone was all old-fashioned about marrying for love alone and that sort of thing. And apparently Charles Linton smiled in that outrageous way of his—you know the way he does—and said quite deliberately, "What a charming luxury! I wish I could delude myself into the same idealistic outlook, but being an ambitious and selfish creature, I shall marry—quite frankly—for money."'

Tina laughed unwillingly, because she could quite imagine Charles saying something absurd like that.

'He wouldn't mean it seriously,' she pointed out to her young companion tolerantly. 'He was joking.'

'Eileen didn't think he was joking,' Audrey retorted darkly. 'And Eileen's very seldom wrong about a man.'

'And on the strength of this flippant statement'—Tina was amusedly incredulous—'Eileen plunged into hospital life?'

'I've told you—you can't imagine how determined Eileen is about anything she really wants.'

'She must be,' Tina agreed, and she stood up, to indicate that this interesting discussion on the joint future of Eileen and Charles Linton was really at an end.

'Oh—are you going?'

'I'm afraid I must.' Tina made that firm.

'Oh, I'm sorry. I was hoping you'd stay and meet Eileen. I'm expecting her any minute, as a matter of fact. She's off duty today.'

Tina could hardly have explained why, but a genuine aversion to meeting the much-discussed Eileen took possession of her, and she merely repeated her assertion that she must go with even greater emphasis.

The whole incident had suddenly become distasteful and more than a little absurd. She had no wish to know anything further of the designs which this girl's sister had on Charles. No doubt the incident was highly coloured by young Audrey's way of dramatising most things. But, even allowing for that, the whole thing left a nasty taste in one's mouth.

With a firm goodbye she escaped upstairs to her room, and putting on her coat, she decided to go out. She had some vague idea about making inquiries and trying to find some way in which she could get a job, though of course there was nothing definite that she could do until her affairs with the lawyers were settled and her identity—one way or the other—was established.

As she reached the lift she saw it already disappearing, and she decided to walk down the stairs instead of waiting. When she turned the last corner of the stairs, an irresistible impulse made her look over into the lounge—and there, talking to young Audrey, was unquestionably the determined Eileen.

Not that there was much family likeness between the two sisters, Tina noticed. At least, not at that distance. But Audrey's air of bravado and ingratiation was very much that of an uncrushable younger sister towards one who made life somewhat difficult. Tina felt a sympathetic smile twitch the corners of her mouth as she watched for a few seconds.

The other girl was undeniably attractive, though she was not wasting much in the way of smiling attraction on her young sister. She was slim and dark and—for a girl of middle height—indescribably elegant. She wore her simple, expensive clothes well.

'Hm! I don't know that I give so much for Charles' chances after all,' reflected Tina—and told herself that she was amused.

But as she stepped out into the sunshine, she found suddenly that she was not amused—that she didn't find Eileen a joke, after all. Not even a bad joke. It was no business of hers, of course, who tried to marry Charles— nor even who succeeded. But she just hated the whole idea.

She had not quite decided why, when Earle Morrison turned the corner of the street and greeted her with a cheerful wave of his hand.

'Hello there! I thought I'd just come around and make sure you were all right after last night.'

'Last night?'

'That Charles took you home safely.'

'Yes, of course.'

'Am I going to have the pleasure of taking you to lunch?' he went on.

Impossible to stand out against so much friendly good will—or to try to decide whether this were good or bad policy. Tina threw doubts and caution to the wind, and went off to enjoy her lunch with Earle.

He took her to some pleasant, exclusive little place where

the food was good and the atmosphere ideal for talking.

'Aren't you and I spending rather a lot of our time just idling about and enjoying nice meals?' Tina said with a smile as she sat down opposite him.

'At the moment—yes,' he agreed. 'But when we both settle just what we're going to do, I guess we shan't be having much of this idling about that seems to worry you. An occasional lunch and a hasty exchange of news will about cover it.'

'I hope so. At least, not about the few chances of meeting, of course. Just that I'd like to get a job.'

He smiled reflectively.

'No great urge to do nursing?'

'Under Charles, you mean?'

'I didn't say so.' Earle smiled reflectively. 'But how *would* you like working under him?'

'I'd loathe it,' Tina replied promptly.

'No—really?' Earle seemed astonished and concerned. 'Don't you like Charles?'

'In a way—yes, of course. But not to work under.'

'Why not?'

'For one thing, he'd be deadly superior. He would always be cheerfully right, and I'm afraid "admiring chorus" is not my best rôle.'

'I think you do Charles an injustice, you know! I know one or two people who worked with him, and they all liked him and thought well of him.'

'I dare say.' Tina was rather contrite by now, and a little surprised to find she had been sb hot about the question. She realised that her unkind reference to 'admiring chorus' probably arose more from an acid recollection of Miss Unsworth than from anything Charles had said or done. 'I'm probably just being the horrid critical relation,' she explained to Earle with a smile, 'refusing to accord the prophet honour in his own family circle.'

'Maybe.' Earle smiled too, but doubtfully. 'But I believe, all the same, that you *don't* like Charles very much, for some reason or other.'

'I don't know him very well yet,' Tina protested. But Earle brushed that aside.

'I suppose it's his positive manner that offends you. Charles always knows so darned well just what he wants.'

'Yes,' Tina said, recalling, slightly against her will, the sidelight which Audrey Unsworth had firmly shed on him. 'He does know his own mind almost ruthlessly well, doesn't he?'

'Ruthlessly?' Earle's eyebrows went up.

'Well——' Tina hesitated. Then she said abruptly, 'I heard something not very—likeable about him today. I suppose that was what made me rather catty just now. Apparently he says—or rather he did say once—that he quite frankly intends to marry for money. That isn't a very nice thing for a man to say outright.'

'But you're quite willing to believe that Charles said it?'

'Well,' Tina admitted, 'perhaps I shouldn't, except for the fact——' She stopped, and suddenly looked very directly at her companion. 'Don't you think it's somehow in character?'

Earle laughed, but a trifle uncomfortably, she thought.

'Look here,' he said protestingly, 'are you asking me this as his friend, or his disapproving cousin, or'—he cocked a quizzical eyebrow—'merely as a young woman who has just inherited quite a tidy fortune?'

CHAPTER SIX

TINA stared at Earle in astonishment for a moment. Then the first thing she thought of saying was:

'Who told *you* I'd "inherited quite a tidy fortune"?'

'Well—Charles did, as a matter of fact.' Earle laughed, but the slightly uncomfortable air deepened.

'He seems pretty free with his information about——'

'No—really. We weren't indulging quite so outrageously in gossip, though I know *it* sounds like it. I don't think he meant to tell me, in quite so many words. It was that first evening—just after we had left you at the air terminal. It was quite natural we should speak about you and the coincidence of his meeting you at the station. I said—if you'll pardon the candour—how pretty you were, and Charles laughed and added on the spur of the moment, "Quite a little heiress, too——" '

'Typical Charles,' murmured Tina, but with less annoyance this time, particularly as there was quite a pleading expression in Earle's nice, worried eyes.

'He didn't mean anything offensive,' Earle hastened to assure her. 'But of course, I expressed a little natural curiosity and he—well, he——' His voice trailed off in some dismay, and Tina saw with amusement that he had recollected Charles' exact words and—quite palpably— they were not very suitable for repetition.

'Yes? Do tell me what he said.'

She smiled mischievously, and Earle rumpled up his hair worriedly.

'The devil of it is that you'll probably take offence again,' he said ruefully. 'I wish I'd never started the subject.'

70

'No, I won't.' She laughed outright. 'I'm beginning to be amused, and that means that I can't remain annoyed too. Besides, I'll remember it was a special occasion. After all, two friends meeting after so long—what could they be but frank?'

'You're laughing at us both now, I suppose?'

'A little. But you mustn't mind. Do tell me. He said I was an heiress—adding gratuitously that I was little, which I'm not. You expressed surprise, of course, and he said——?'

'I'm afraid he said—"And well I know it! The little devil's done me out of sixty thousand personally." '

Earle looked so genuinely scared after admitting the unfortunate comment that Tina had to laugh again, though she flushed in her turn.

'Horrid of him! But there is a certain amount of truth in it, as a matter of fact,' she admitted. 'I'm terribly sorry he feels like that, but I do understand it. I wish he'd let me do something about it, but he won't and—— Did he explain the circumstances to you?' Tina asked suddenly.

'Not really.' And Earle looked so much interested, as well as relieved, at her lenient reception of his account, that Tina felt bound to give him an explanation of how it was that she—the stranger from America—had walked in and collected every penny from someone who was supposed only to have known her as a baby.

'Yes, a bit tough for Charles, I admit,' Earle said thoughtfully at the end. 'But there isn't any need why you should feel uncomfortable. Old ladies do these things— particularly old ladies with money, somehow—and a legacy's a legacy, when all's said and done. The old girl was perfectly entitled to leave her money where she pleased, and Charles couldn't ever have had dazzling expectations from her, since the big sum was never involved until after her death.'

'I know, I've thought of all that too,' Tina agreed. 'But it's a pretty maddening position, to hear of a fortune coming into the family and going out again immediately! Par-

ticularly if money means rather a lot—at least, I mean——'
She hesitated. Then she smiled rather quizzically at Earle
in her turn. 'You didn't answer my query about the marrying for money question, you know. You just sidetracked
me.'

'Did I now?' Earle smiled back at her. 'And the query
was——?'

'Just "Do you think Charles is the kind to marry for
money?" I suppose.'

'I can imagine him doing so.'

'In cold blood?'

Earle wrinkled his forehead in some perplexity.

'I don't think Charles has ever had his affections aroused
at all, you know,' was what he said. 'It isn't that he's cold-
hearted or cold-blooded, or whatever you like to call it. Not
at all. He's a good friend and a marvellous doctor, and you
can't be either of those unless you've got real feeling. But
I'm sure he's never been in love with anyone—to use the
standard phrase—and Charles is very much inclined to be
amused by anything he has never had to take seriously.'

'I've noticed that,' murmured Tina.

'And until someone really bowls him over, I can quite
imagine he would half laughingly assure himself that it was
wiser to marry for solid material advantage than for any
romantic mirage.'

'And even do it?'

Earle shrugged.

'Why shouldn't a man act according to his views—even
if they're mistaken views?'

'Hm—and find out the mistake too late?'

He laughed.

'I guess some of them never find it out,' he said, slightly
emphasising his drawl.

Tina didn't say anything to that. She was thinking hard
about Charles Linton. Earle was right, she thought. It
wasn't that Charles didn't possess feelings—he had never
had them roused. Well, one could only hope that no
predatory Eileen would catch him before the rousing pro-

cess had taken place. Pity that sixty thousand hadn't come to him. It would have placed him beyond the temptation to do anything as silly as marry for money. One always came back to that, reflected Tina with a sigh. And she was glad when Earle turned the conversation to another subject.

During the next few days Tina saw nothing of her supposed cousin—but she thought about him a good deal, all the same. Then at the end of that week as she came into the hotel the clerk at the desk said:

'Oh, Miss Frayne, I am glad to see you. There's a gentleman waiting for you. He's telephoned I don't know how many times, and now he's in the lounge writing a note to you because we didn't know when you would be back.'

'A gentleman?' Tina repeated rather vaguely. And then: 'Oh, heavens! It's Earle, I suppose. I ought to have let him know——'

She went at once into the lounge. But the man who got up from the writing-table and came to meet her with an expression of almost angry anxiety was not Earle. It was Charles.

'Charles!' she began. But he took hold of her by her arms and exclaimed very rudely:

'Good God, girl! Where have you been?'

'Out—out sightseeing,' stammered Tina, suddenly finding her lips unsteady. And then for some reason or other he kissed her.

'Couldn't you have let me know?' he said, but more gently. 'You've been out every time I rang the hotel.'

'Not very well. You see, I—I——'

'Yes, that's all right.' He had his arm round her now, and leading her over to the settee, he made her sit down, and had hot coffee brought for her and sandwiches.

'Get outside that,' he ordered. And she did—very thankfully.

'Enjoying yourself?' he inquired laconically when he apparently judged she felt more like talking.

She nodded. 'It's marvellous to see all the places I'd heard about.' In her character of Sonia—Tina remembered just in time that she was not supposed to know London.

'It's a great city.' He smiled at her—not as though he were amused, but as though something pleased him—perhaps because he was relieved at seeing her.

'Have you been very busy, Charles?'

'Yes. A couple of emergency cases came up and I've had a lot of work on besides.'

'Yes, of course, I suppose so.'

'I couldn't get along here before today. I telephoned several times, but the girl on the switchboard couldn't say anything more intelligent than that you'd gone out two or three days ago and not come back.'

'Oh, I'm sorry, Charles. I did leave a message at the desk to say where I'd gone.'

'Yes, I got it when I came here today.'

'I've been out every day at crack of dawn and not got back until late.'

'So I gathered. You must be tired. I won't keep you any longer.'

She stood up.

'Charles, it was nice of you to—to worry so much.'

He smiled at her, and suddenly his dark eyes were very bright and unexpectedly kindly.

'Well, you're all the family I've got,' he pointed out lightly.

'Was that why you kissed me when you first saw me?' she asked, a little stupidly because she felt so dead with sleepiness.

'That?—oh, that was just an emotional outburst.'

'That doesn't sound a bit like you.' She smiled faintly.

'It isn't,' he assured her coolly. 'Put it down to a sort of angry relief.'

She thought at first she would stay to ask him—Why 'angry'? But, on second thoughts, she decided she would rather sleep.

'Goodnight, Charles. Thanks awfully for coming to see about me.'

'Goodnight, my dear.'

She smiled up at him—with sleepy vagueness, she couldn't help feeling. And he coolly and firmly kissed her once more.

'Not another emotional outburst, surely?' Tina murmured. ·

'No. Just because you looked up at me at the correct moment—and you're a good, worthwhile little cousin.'

'I'm *not* specially little.' It seemed enormously important that this matter should be set right. But he only laughed and said:

'Go along to bed.'

And because it seemed the very nicest thing on earth to do, Tina did.

In the next week or two Tina grew very much used to setting a hectic pace of sightseeing. Since, until Mr Medway straightened out the legal side of things, she could not set about finding herself a place to live or a job, Tina resigned herself to filling in her time as best she could, renewing her acquaintance with places and buildings that she had known before. Occasionally she had lunch or a leisurely dinner with Earle. But he was busy with his work now and had little time.

'Have you seen anything of Charles lately?' he asked her over coffee one day.

'Not since just after the first week-end. He appeared at my hotel then, overcome with emotion and family responsibility, intent on bullying me or kissing me—and ending by doing both.'

'Charles did!'

'Yes.' She smiled mischievously. 'Which bit surprises you more?'

'We-ell, I must confess that the whole description is intriguingly out of character. Why did he want to kiss you?'

'Oh, Earle! How ungallant!'

'Well, I mean—why, apart from the fact that any man would want to kiss anything as sweet and pretty as you?'

'A noble—if slightly overdone—recovery,' Tina told him. 'As a matter of fact, there's a distressingly prosaic explanation. He'd been phoning the hotel for news of me for two or three days, and the idiot of a phone girl went no further than to report that I'd gone out a few days before and not returned. I suppose he thought I was dead, and experienced a cousinly relief on finding me still alive.'

Earle didn't answer that, but stared at her so reflectively that after a moment she said:

'Well?'

'I was just thinking—that isn't sufficient in itself to explain Charles kissing you. I should have thought he would be much more likely to shake you.'

'He did that first,' Tina said. Whereat Earle laughed.

'He must be a good deal attached to you, after all, my dear.'

'On the strength of one shake and one kiss?' said Tina, remembering then that it had been two kisses, but seeing no reason why she should give Earle that added information.

'No. On the strength of so much apparently genuine anxiety for you.'

'Why shouldn't he be anxious about me?' Tina smiled. 'As he himself remarked, I am all the family he has.'

'But a mere cousin—whom he's known for something less than a week.'

'Earle, you aren't in a very flattering mood today, are you? After all, it wasn't like expressing anxiety over a cold or a headache. He thought I'd gone under a bus or something. I feel even the uncaring Charles may be allowed a few qualms.'

'And suppose you *had* been dead—purely for the sake of argument, of course——'

'Oh, of course. Don't mind my feelings.'

Earle grinned.

'I was going to say—in that case. I presume the famous "tidy fortune" would have come to friend Charles?'

'Why, Earle!' She looked astonished and impressed. 'I suppose it would. Yes—that *was* rather nice and disinterested of him to be so worried about me, in those circumstances. Though, as a matter of fact, I don't expect he gave that aspect a thought.'

'Think not?'

'Do you?'

'It seems a bit superhuman not to let the idea even cross one's mind, however regretfully,' Earle murmured reflectively. 'Particularly if one needed money badly.'

'But does—does *Charles* need money badly? What for? I had no idea!'

'Oh, I didn't mean that he's in any financial embarrassment. Only that he's full of some scheme that would take the deuce of a lot of money to carry out.'

'Earle, do tell me! I didn't know anything about this.'

'No? Well, I don't expect there's any harm in my talking about it. I suppose he would have told you about it himself sooner or later.'

Tina privately supposed *not*, remembering Charles' amused but emphatic refusal to let her 'come to an arrangement' with him about her inheritance. He would hardly be likely to choose her as confidante for any plan which needed money.

'Well, tell me,' she urged.

'It's all connected with—or rather, an extension of—his work, of course,' Earle explained, as he lit their cigarettes and, pushing aside the coffee-cups, leaned his arms on the table. 'You'll understand that in this business of— well, practically re-making people who've been badly disfigured, there's a psychological, as well as a physical, problem to consider.'

Tina nodded, her interested gaze fixed on Earle.

'Sometimes, even when a patient has been entirely restored, there's a question of getting him—or, even more often, her—used to ordinary life again. There isn't always this problem, of course. Some people are quite wonderful about it, and take the whole thing in their stride. But there *are* cases where the thing that's most needed is a sort of transition stage between hospital life and their own everyday life again.'

'Yes, I can understand that. I think I should need it,' Tina said.

Earle smiled and shrugged.

'Maybe. It's a question of temperament—and also the kind of home to which the patient is returning. And another problem is that quite often this plastic work has to be done in several stages, and there isn't any reason why, in between, the patient shouldn't return home and have a normal, non-hospital existence. In fact, it's far the best thing, if the home is a suitable—what you might call a "sympathetic"—home.'

'But they aren't all?'

'No—exactly. They aren't all. Charles' idea is that he wants to run his own place. Not exactly a convalescent home and not exactly a rest home, but a place where any specially difficult case can, so to speak, learn to come back to normal life again.'

'Oh, Earle! That's rather a super idea! He'd be so good at it too. There's something—bracing as well as understanding about Charles.' And then she stopped, a little surprised, because she had realised that she based this view of him on nothing more than his attitude to her when she had come in worn out and dispirited.

However, Earle seemed to agree with her.

'I think so too,' he said. 'Of course he wouldn't have a great deal to do with the actual running of the place—he's too busy on operational work—but I think he has quite a lot of the details settled in his own mind already. The kind of person he wants to run the place, and so on. The only snag is—he has nothing like enough capital, poor old Charles!'

'Oh, Earle!'

'So that brings us right back to my previous shameful assertion that it would be somewhat superhuman not even to think what one *would* do if a charming, but not very well-known, cousin no longer stood in the way of a handsome inheritance.'

'Earle, you are absurd! You talk like the prologue to a

murder mystery. But I know what you mean. Oh, I wish the money were his!'

That came from the bottom of her heart, but it only had the effect of making Earle laugh.

'Oh, come! That's a bit too disinterested, isn't it?' he protested, and Tina realised that she was not keeping a sufficient guard on her tongue. Her exclamation must have sounded distinctly overdone to anyone who had no idea of the true state of things.

She laughed nervously, and said quickly:

'Oh, I meant that I wished I could help. Perhaps I can. I must think it over.' And then she firmly changed the subject.

But that night she thought and thought of Charles and his wonderful idea and the money which *should* have been his to carry out that idea.

'It's like cheating not only Charles himself but all those people who so tragically need his help,' Tina thought wretchedly. 'If only——'

And then there came into Tina's mind—at least, she always thought afterwards that it must have been at just that moment—the beginning of a wonderful idea of her own.

Why should she not finance this project of Charles'? She could represent it as her contribution to a deserving cause —that much at least of undeserved credit she would have to accept—and then Charles could have no idea that she was trying to force money on him personally.

It was true that, if she became involved like this, she would have to remain Sonia Frayne for an indefinite period —at least until the money had all gone, she thought recklessly—but somehow that hardly mattered now. She would be making that money do what it *should* be doing—spending it as Charles himself would have spent it, had he known it was really his. The complete abstract justice of that seemed more important to Tina than any risks or difficulties. And—perhaps for the first time since she had taken Sonia's passport from the drawer—she experienced a feeling of extreme peace and content.

As though Fate were playing deliberately into her hands, Tina had a telephone call from Charles the very next day, and the inquiry which he had to make, in that abrupt, incisive tone of his—so different from Earle's drawl—was: Had she the afternoon free, by any chance, and would she like to spend it with him?

'Charles, I'd love to!' she exclaimed, a little more eagerly than the invitation warranted.

'Good. Do you want to go anywhere special, or would you rather have a lazy afternoon after your strenuous time in the last few weeks? We could drive out into Surrey, if you like, and have tea somewhere down the river. We don't have to go far, but I know a nice place.'

'It sounds very attractive, Charles.'

'Very well. I'll guarantee to get you back for an early dinner.'

And he rang off, leaving her to wonder pleasurably whether the early dinner was to be with him too.

He arrived that afternoon—punctual to the minute, as she had rather expected—in a slightly battered sports car, which proved, however, to be unexpectedly comfortable.

As he handed Tina in, he glanced with amused appreciation at her leaf-brown suit and the soft green scarf that was tied round her fair hair.

'I feel that my ancient car should at least have had a new coat of paint in your honour,' he told her. 'You're looking very charming, my little cousin.'

'Well, I feel a washed-out rag.'

'An exceptionally attractive rag,' he assured her, and she laughed.

She thought, as she settled back contentedly in her seat, that he was looking very nice himself in a light grey suit which emphasised his unusually warm colouring. She liked that clear, dark tan, and she noticed again with appreciation that his fine, clever hands, which held the wheel so confidently, were the same even brown.

After the first conventional inquiries and answers had

been exchanged they lapsed into comfortable silence, and Tina reflected idly that Charles could be restful as well as provocative. Perhaps he was intentionally giving her a chance to relax. At any rate, whatever the reason, he was certainly allowing her to enjoy the beautiful afternoon, the unaccustomed leisure, and his own company without making any demands upon her.

Indeed, Tina was inclined to think afterwards that she had actually almost fallen asleep when suddenly she came back to consciousness with a start, and to the realisation that the car was slowing down. Charles was not looking at her. He was looking away to the left of the car with a slight frown of extreme concentration. And as Tina's gaze followed his, she saw through a gap in the trees a square, sturdy, altogether enchanting house.

A short gravel drive led up to a wide, porticoed doorway, with a knocker so large and so bright that even from where she was Tina could see how the light shone back from it. On either side of the doorway spread the many-windowed front, absolutely balanced, in perfect regularity, which was somehow amusing and endearing.

'Charles, what a marvellous house!'

He glanced at her amusedly and said:

'Oh, you *are* awake?'

'Of course.' She had the usual unreasonable desire to insist that she had not been asleep, but there was something more important just then. 'It's ideal!'

'What is ideal?'

'Why, the house, of course.' She was too much excited and too near sleep still to think much what she was saying.

'Ideal for what?'

'Why, for your—my—I suppose *our* purpose. Oh, Charles, I hadn't explained. I do want you to have your convalescent home. It's a wonderful idea. We—I mean I— couldn't spend the money on anything better. Oh, I'm explaining so badly. But you must understand what I mean. Don't you think that house would do marvellously?'

She paused breathlessly, but he didn't answer.

He was silent so long that she began to see the absurdity of her outburst.

'Well, one—one couldn't tell from this distance, of course. We—one would have to go over it—perhaps another house would be better——' Her voice trailed away into the silence which was becoming so embarrassing.

He looked at her with those bright, speculative eyes of his, and she saw that he was smiling very slightly. She was enormously relieved, and she exclaimed:

'Oh, you're not—angry, are you?—or embarrassed?'

'No,' he said slowly. 'I'm not angry and I'm certainly not embarrassed. I was only wondering——'

'Yes, Charles?' She bit her lip with anxiety.

'—What you would say if I asked you to marry me.'

CHAPTER SEVEN

'MARRY you?' repeated Tina slowly. 'But—there isn't any need for that.'

It sounded a particularly silly comment to her, when she had made it, and it certainly seemed to cause Charles some amusement.

'Need? No, I don't imagine there is any *need* exactly. But then it wasn't necessity, my dear, that prompted the suggestion.'

'What did then?' Tina felt impelled to ask, while at the back of her mind she was wondering if anyone had ever received quite such an odd proposal before.

'First, I suppose, your sensational offer to finance my convalescent home,' he admitted slowly, 'and then the very obvious fact that for us to marry would be quite the simplest and most satisfactory way of carrying out the suggestion.'

'I don't think it would be anything of the sort,' Tina replied, a trifle tartly. 'I should call it complicating things quite unnecessarily.'

He turned to face her then, putting his arm along the back of the seat, and she noticed that his eyes were dancing, and she could not suppress a suspicion that at this moment he was taking life even less seriously than usual.

'And I don't think this is a very good joke,' she said firmly.

'My dear girl, it would be a frightful joke—and in the worst of taste—if it were intended for a joke. But it's not. I'm perfectly serious.'

'About wanting to marry me?'

'About wanting to marry you.'

She looked into his eyes and said:

'I don't think I altogether believe that.'

Whereupon he took her in his arms and kissed her and said:

'You're rather a little goose, then. But quite the most attractive goose possible.'

'The kind that lays golden eggs, in fact,' Tina retorted somewhat caustically, because she was annoyed to find how very much she liked being kissed by him.

'Of course,' he assured her lightly. 'Don't you realise that I'm trying to marry you for your money?'

'Charles, can't you be serious for just one minute?'

'I am serious—I've told you so.'

And suddenly she saw that he was.

'And you're seriously asking me to marry you, for the sole reason that you think you—we—can run your convalescent home better that way?'

'That's not the sole reason.' He smiled down at her. 'There are—as there should be for all great decisions—a variety of reasons.'

'Perhaps you wouldn't mind telling me about some of the others?' Tina said, a little dryly.

'Not at all. What shall I put first? That I like you very much, I think.'

'It is quite important,' Tina murmured.

'Second, that you like me very much——'

'How do you know I do?' Tina demanded quickly.

'If you're prepared to deny it, I'll try to believe you,' he told her.

She looked at her big, handsome cousin—who was not her cousin, of course, when one came to think about it—and she knew with a sudden sensation not unlike alarm how very much she did like him.

'No.' Her eyes fell unaccountably. 'We'll let that pass.'

'Good.' He lightly touched her cheek with those strong brown fingers of his. 'Next, let me remind you that you are the innocent and appropriate heiress of fiction while I am the mercenary creature on the lookout for a rich and credulous wife.'

She laughed irresistibly and said: 'You're quite absurd!'

'Oh no. I'm merely giving much more serious thought to the important question of matrimony than most men do. Weighing the pros and cons seems to me a much more likely way to happiness than taking romantic headers into unknown waters.'

She didn't answer that at once, because she was hardly listening. What she was thinking was that here, in this half-absurd, half-serious proposal of marriage, lay the real solution to the problem of letting Charles have the handling of his own legacy.

'Of course it *would* mean that the money became yours at last,' she murmured, more to herself than to him.

'My dear child, it wouldn't mean anything of the sort,' he assured her briskly. 'It would still be yours. You seem to be in a perpetual state of trying to hand on your fortune to someone else.'

'Not at all!' Tina was a good deal frightened to find she had so clearly revealed her true feelings. 'Only you said you were trying to marry me for my money,' she reminded him. 'I naturally thought——'

'Yes, of course you did. I understand.' And he actually kissed her lightly again.

'Don't you think you're kissing me rather a lot, considering I haven't said that I'll marry you?' Tina inquired.

'That was just a cousinly kiss,' he assured her. And she immediately found herself wondering—with something like pleasurable excitement—what kind of kiss he would give her if she did say 'yes'.

'And what,' he inquired, 'does that extremely sober look mean?'

'I was thinking.'

'About me?'

'In a way—yes. But don't be so self-satisfied. I was wondering what I should have said if—if you'd made this offer sensibly and less—less frivolously.'

'You would have turned me down flat, my dear,' he assured her promptly. 'And richly should I have deserved it.'

'Oh, Charles——' She laughed protestingly. But she made no protest when he drew her against him and looked down at her more seriously.

'You think I don't mean all this, don't you?' he said.

'I—don't know quite what to think,' Tina admitted rather helplessly. 'I can't imagine that anyone suggested marriage in quite this weird way before.'

'But you won't turn it down on that alone?' He was quite grave now. 'I do want to marry you, Sonia.' She started at the unfamiliar name. 'That is true from the bottom of my heart.'

She looked at him then, and if her smile was quizzical, it was rather sweet too.

'I don't think your heart has much to do with it, Charles,' she said.

'As much of it as ever rules my head,' he assured her lightly. 'Please say you'll marry me.'

She didn't think the plea came very easily from him. He was much more used to insisting. But there was urgency in the pressure of the arm which held her. He did want to marry her. For whatever reasons—and Tina admitted that, even now, these were not particularly clear—he did want to marry her. And she——?

Tina tried not to think how attractive she found that dark, imperious face which was so near to hers. His sheer animal attraction and the compelling force of his personality must not be allowed to have anything to do with her decision, because—for whatever reason he wished to marry her—it certainly was not that he loved her, and therefore she must not lose her head about him.

Wise decision—but how singularly difficult to put into execution! Particularly in the last half-hour. Try as she would to remember that the really important things were the return of the legacy to Charles, the certainty that his work should go on unhampered, the relinquishing of a position which she had so dishonestly acquired—she knew that the thought which was really swaying her resolution was:

This is the most impossible and wonderful and overwhelming thing that has ever happened to me! If I go with him I shall often be angry and sometimes afraid, but I shall never again be without colour and warmth and the wonderful flame of his vitality. This hasn't anything to do with it, of course, but——

'I'll marry you, Charles,' she said in a small, firm voice which she hardly recognised for her own. And then he kissed her, and she knew that when he had said, 'I'm very fond of you,' he had stated the exact truth. He was not less than 'fond' of her—and certainly no more.

It was he who should really have shattered the moment first with his instinctive distrust of anything purely romantic, but in point of fact it was she who, having returned his kiss, said:

'And now shall we go and look at the house?'

She thought for a moment that there was something faintly disconcerted about his laugh. Or perhaps it was only that she puzzled him a little. At any rate, his answer came promptly enough.

'You think of everything, my dear—and in the right order. You'll make the perfect doctor's wife.'

Tina said nothing to that, possibly because she was startled to hear herself described, in so many words, as anyone's wife.

They drove slowly up the well-kept drive. Evidently the place had not been empty long enough to fall into disrepair, and certainly the brightness of the knocker and the many windows suggested that the caretaker had a serious regard for the cordial invitation 'to view at any time' which adorned the notice-board, stating that the place was for sale.

A knock at the bright knocker brought a diminutive, bustling little woman in black to the door, and her whole efficient manner indicated that, at whatever eccentric time one had chosen 'to view', she would have been ready and prepared for the inspection.

'You want to view the house,' she said, more as a statement than a question, and it was borne in on Tina that this was not the first time that Charles had been here.

As the little woman in black led the way across the hall, Tina slipped her arm into Charles' and pulled him back beside her.

'Did you bring me here on purpose today?' she asked somewhat dryly. But he glanced down at her with unusually boyish honesty and shook his head.

'No. I can't keep away from the place,' he stated quite simply. 'I suppose I just chose this way because I always like to take the chance of passing and making sure that no one else has bought it yet.'

'I see.' Tina felt her lips twitch with an irresistible smile. Just so must he have flattened a schoolboy nose against shop-windows long ago while he coveted a train or a Meccano set for Christmas. It was a nice, ingenuous streak she had not thought of discovering in Charles, and her heart warmed to him the more.

They 'viewed' the house with a thoroughness dictated by their guide as much as by their own inclination. She had no intention that any of its beauties should be overlooked, and she determinedly regaled them with the full history of its late owners, a certain 'Sir Thomas and his lady'.

'Brought her here as a bride, he did, on the day our present Queen was born,' the one-time housekeeper explained with a sigh. 'Ah, that was a happy day, that was.'

Tina didn't like to ask whether its happiness was due to the birth of our present Queen or the advent of Sir Thomas and his bride, so she murmured something sympathetic which could pass for either agreement or mere comment.

But on the subject of the house itself she could be—and was—unreservedly enthusiastic.

It was roomy and gracious and almost amusingly cheerful. Tina felt she could hardly have imagined a more delightful place for harassed or nervous people trying to regain their emotional balance after illness. Incidentally—and she supposed as a somewhat secondary consideration—she could not have imagined a place where she herself would have more readily decided to live.

That was—if she and Charles *were* going to live here too.

She glanced at him, wondering quite how she could put that question, and as she did so, he took her arm in his turn, as though he wished to engage her very special attention.

'You see how this small wing is more or less shut away from the rest of the house?'

'Yes?'

'Well, we could have our quarters there—really like a flat of our own.'

'Yes,' Tina said again. And for the first time—or so it seemed to her—she realised that she had indeed committed herself to marrying Charles, to living with him—here in this very house probably. The whole thing was suddenly real and clear-cut. She was, she supposed, a fiancée, looking over her future home.

By the time they left, Tina had made up her mind that the house should be theirs. It seemed an afternoon for quick and improbable decisions, and if she could decide on the spur of the moment to do anything so mad as marry Charles, there was surely nothing incongruous in deciding to buy a large country house within twenty-five miles of London.

Besides, the real point was—that Charles' *own* money would be used for Charles' especial pleasure.

Over tea they discussed details. Whether the price of the house were reasonable (which it was)—how long it would take to furnish the place—what staff would be needed, and so on.

Tina began to wonder if she had always more or less hankered after just such a project as this, or whether it was simply that Charles had the faculty of imparting his own enthusiasm to anyone he wished to interest.

Once or twice she experienced a flat, left-out-in-the-cold sensation, because it *was* a little disconcerting that one's fiancé—if she could ever think of Charles like that—should seem so much more interested in his future home than his future bride.

She was not aware of having given away her feelings in her manner. But there was not much that Charles' observant eyes missed, and on the way home he suddenly said, as though continuing a conversation they had already started:

'And at this point, of course, you're feeling a bit dismayed?'

She smiled slightly.

'I shouldn't put it at "dismayed", Charles.'

'A little worried then—wondering if you have been stampeded into some crazy project which doesn't promise much for you personally.'

'And have I?' she queried, a trifle dryly. 'Been stampeded, I mean, into the crazy project, etc?'

He gave her an unusually troubled glance, and drove on in silence for a few moments. Then he said rather carefully:

'If you feel I am behaving—badly or unfairly over this, you can still withdraw, you know.'

'And leave your beautiful project in ruins?'

'The convalescent home is not the only thing to be considered.' He appeared to be deeply concerned with his driving.

'No?'

'No, of course not.'

'I'm not so sure of the "of course not",' she told him, but not unkindly. 'There is one question I want to ask, and I should like a plain and unbantering reply to it.'

'You shall have it.'

'Is your chief reason for marrying me the fact that you can have your convalescent home that way?'

'The plain and unbantering reply to that is—No.'

She was conscious of a genuine and pleasurable surprise at that—and she smiled a little grimly to find she was so easily pleased.

'But if I had *not* had the money——?'

'Must you ask that one?'

'It's a rather obvious continuation of the first question. But I'll change it if you like. What *is* your chief reason for wanting to marry me?'

'The fact that I like you enormously.'

She wondered, almost dispassionately, if he were afraid of the word 'love' or deliberately avoided it. Aloud she said:

'But not enough to marry me without the money, I take it?' She found that she could smile rather quizzically about that, and it seemed that it was his turn to be serious. She saw his mouth set obstinately.

'Do you want the brutal truth?'

'The brutal truth,' she assured him.

'Then I'm damned if I'll marry anyone without enough money to help found my home, but'—and suddenly that almost irresistible smile of his flashed out—'I'm extraordinarily glad that you happen to be the one with it.'

'I see.' Tina nodded with a reflective smile. 'Then I may regard myself more or less as a sugared pill—the sugar perfectly satisfactory, and the pill not so bad when one gets to it?'

She laughed. But he didn't. In fact, with an unexpectedly troubled expression, he drew the car to a standstill by the side of the road.

'We've got this all on a wrong basis somewhere.'

'Have we?'

'You know we have. It's my fault. I thought I could carry it off with a light hand—that if I did it with all solemnity, the whole thing would sound too fantastic for acceptance.'

'But then you are a little afraid of serious things, Charles, aren't you?' she said quietly. 'In anything but your work, I mean.'

'No.' He frowned doubtfully. 'I don't think so. I don't think I'm exactly afraid of anything.'

She laughed at that and said, quite irrelevantly:

'Charles, you must have been a nice little boy.'

'Why?' He smiled then, but the doubtful expression remained.

'Why? Oh, I couldn't explain just now. It would take too long. Besides, we were talking of something more vital. The fact that, on reflection, you don't much like the way you handled your proposal.'

'No—I should think not. Do you?'

'Not at all.'

'Hm. In fact, I succeeded in sounding extremely implausible——'

'You did.'

'—While you, if I'm not much mistaken, extracted an unnecessary amount of amusement from the whole thing.'

She smiled demurely and said:

'What do you want to do about it? Begin all over again?'

His laughing eyes met hers, and he nodded.

'Just that. Sonia—I wish you had another name, but you haven't, so it can't be helped—I think you're a darling, and have quite the nicest sense of humour I have ever come across. I wish you would marry me, because you would be a delightful person to live with——'

'Be honest! Don't forget the money!'

'I'm coming to that. But because I am a one-idea man, with a fanatical passion for my work, I must marry someone who can help me——'

'Financially?'

'Well, of course, financially. I don't need any other kind of help with my work,' he assured her promptly. 'But because of—what I said—it *is* terribly important, too, that you have money.'

'Go on—finish it. "And in fact you wouldn't have asked me if I hadn't had it."'

'I'm not going to put that into words,' he said, with a touch of unexpected firmness. And at that she laughed and laughed.

He took her in his arms with a suddenness which seemed to surprise him as much as her.

'Why are you laughing?'

'Because I have the nicest sense of humour, of course.'

He kissed her—once or twice—not at all as he had kissed her before.

'Will you marry me, darling?'

'Yes, of course.'

'Why?' The question was abrupt, and he held her a little away from him, so that he could look at her.

'Because I think you're a darling, and have the nicest sense of humour—though one wouldn't think so at the moment—and *might* be delightful to live with, and——'

'You little devil,' he said slowly, smiling so that there seemed a light behind his dark eyes. 'You're still laughing at me, aren't you?'

'Do you mind?'

'No,' he admitted slowly. 'I like it to a ridiculous degree. And now I think we'll drive on.'

Which they did, at a good pace, until they reached the outskirts of London once more.

She was faintly surprised that even later, over dinner, he made no inquiries about her choice of an engagement ring or her ideas for their wedding. The smaller, picturesque details seemed to hold little interest for him.

'And I shouldn't be very much surprised,' reflected Tina without rancour, 'if he forgot altogether about getting me a ring.'

But when he left her that evening there was something extremely possessive, she thought, about his goodnight kiss. He was not prepared—or even qualified, she supposed —to play the romantic lover, but he certainly considered that she had become very much his affair. And that perhaps was all one could expect from a man of Charles' temperament.

When he had gone and she was alone at last, Tina went almost immediately to her room, anxious to think over quietly the extraordinary developments of the day.

But she found that, even alone, and with no more to distract her attention than the unexciting surroundings of a conventional hotel bedroom, she was still quite unable to think of the new situation in clear-cut terms.

Certainly she had solved the problem of how to arrange that at least part of Charles' money should be spent as he wished. So much at any rate was clear—and it soothed her conscience considerably to reflect on that. But in arranging that, she had committed herself to spending the rest of her life—or, on the most cynical estimate, a part of her life— in his company.

By all the usual arguments she should have been dismayed by the prospect. And she was not. *That* was the part she found so hard to realise.

'I suppose,' Tina told herself, 'Charles is the kind of man one could fall in love with rather easily.'

And that was the nearest she came to admitting that she *had* fallen in love with him, and that she was both scared and entranced by the thought of marrying him.

Characteristically, although he put in no appearance the next day, she received no loving message either by telephone or post. Evidently he was not going to pretend to any feelings he did not possess. If the casual affection— cousinly or otherwise—which he had for her was not enough, then she must find it out for herself now, before it was too late.

'He isn't going to be the kind of lover who bores by excessive devotion,' thought Tina, not without amusement. And when he did telephone to her the following morning, she hoped that her tone conveyed a casual self-possession to match his own.

'It's about your ring,' he explained, as though it were necessary to give some reason for having telephoned to her.

'My ring?'

'Yes. Engagement ring, you know. It's customary to have one on these occasions.'

'Oh yes—of course. Did you want to arrange to come

up to town and help me choose it?' She knew that he was speaking from the hospital just outside London where most of his work was done.

'No, I'm afraid I can't do that.' He sounded faintly absent, as though they were discussing something of minor importance, or as though his thoughts were very much on something else. 'I shall be operating all today and probably tomorrow too. We've had a whole lot of new patients in.'

'I don't mind waiting.'

'Oh—why should you? I thought I would telephone Petersen's in Hatton Garden. They know me there, and you can go in and choose what you like.'

She didn't answer for a moment, and he said:

'Are you there?'

'Oh yes.' Tina suppressed a desire to answer extremely sharply. How could he be so *idiotically* tactless? Fancy walking in and buying your own engagement ring!

'You will be able to find it, won't you?'

'Yes.'

'Is anything wrong?'

'No,' Tina said, with an irony which she hoped travelled over the telephone wires. 'There's nothing wrong.'

He laughed slightly.

'You're marrying a busy surgeon, you know,' he told her.

'I know.' She felt faintly ashamed, though she told herself annoyedly that it was he who should feel ashamed.

'Then that's arranged?' There was hardly any question implied in his tone. 'I hope to be back in town at the beginning of next week. I'll ring you then. Goodbye, my dear. Choose something you really like.'

And before she could say that she was not so sure after all that she *wanted* an engagement ring, he had rung off.

Tina slowly replaced the receiver with a hand that shook slightly—but whether with justifiable anger or small-minded pique she was not quite sure.

'He *is* terribly busy, and it's ridiculous to turn temperamental over personal details when he's doing work that may save people's lives,' she told herself. 'Besides——'

But she couldn't quite face going over what 'besides' covered. It had too much to do with the fact that something which had become romantic and precious to her was nothing more than part of a business arrangement to him. Quite a charming business arrangement, of course—but that was all.

Choosing her ring was not so embarrassing after all, she found. Either the assistant was trained to a perfection of politeness which excluded every trace of curiosity from his manner, or else other busy fiancés had adopted this method of bestowing an engagement ring. The only really interesting point, it seemed, was that she should have exactly what she wanted.

In the end she chose a fiery opal, set in a ring of small diamonds—partly, she told herself, to demonstrate that she was not superstitious, and partly for the rather absurd and romantic reason that the hidden fire in it seemed in keeping with the man who was giving it to her.

'A very beautiful choice,' the assistant assured her, so politely that she wondered if he were going to put it on her finger for her. He refrained, however, and she left the shop with her engagement ring in its elegant little case.

As she entered the hotel again, Audrey Unsworth hailed her.

'I say, do come and have tea with me. Something perfectly frightful has happened!'

'Has it?'

Tina, more accustomed now to Audrey's dramatic way of imparting almost all information, followed her, without any visible signs of alarm.

'Yes.' Audrey sank into the corner of a settee and regarded her with an abnormally solemn expression. 'Do you know that Charles Linton's gone and got himself engaged?'

Tina's hand closed a trifle nervously on the handbag where her ring lay concealed.

'Well—yes, I did know,' she admitted cautiously.

'Then it's true? Lord! I don't know what Eileen will do.'

'I should think,' Tina retorted crisply, 'that there's remarkably little she can do. Except mind her own business.'

'Oh, but you don't under*stand*. It all looked like working out so well. Mr Linton is going to have some sort of convalescent home of his own, and he'd asked Eileen if she would like to come and be one of the nurses on the staff, and——'

'Eileen!'

'Oh yes. And you see it would have been *ideal*. She rang me up and told me all about it this morning. Only the rumour was going the rounds that he'd got engaged too. She didn't know whether to be pleased about the convalescent home or wild about the rumour. I mean, a wife can get so terribly in the *way*, can't she?'

'I hadn't thought of it like that,' Tina admitted, extremely dryly. 'You see, I happen to be going to be the wife in question.'

CHAPTER EIGHT

AUDREY'S pretty mouth positively dropped open, and she stared at Tina with a mixture of amazement and reproach which made Tina feel irritatedly guilty.

'*You're* going to marry Charles Linton? But you *told* me, hardly any time ago, that you weren't engaged or anything, and you sounded as though nothing was further from your thoughts. And now, just because I told you too much about Eileen——'

'Nothing of the sort,' Tina interrupted briskly. 'Please let's have this quite straight. Eileen—or anything you told me about Eileen—had nothing whatever to do with my—my decision.'

'But you told me——'

'Yes, I know I did.' Tina felt it was mean of her to be quite so much annoyed by the repetition. 'It was true then.'

'What was?'

'Well—what you said. That—that nothing was further from my thoughts than'—she coloured slightly—'than marrying Charles.'

'You mean you just suddenly found you'd fallen for each other?' The romance of the situation seemed to mollify Audrey slightly.

'Something like that.' Tina spoke a trifle hastily for one who had been overtaken by sudden romance. 'Anyway, that's how things are now, I'm afraid, and I hope Eileen will realise——'

'Oh, she won't,' Audrey assured her with gloomy positiveness.

'It really isn't her business, you know.' Tina tried to

make that sound sweet-tempered and reasonable, but Audrey obviously thought the objection had little bearing on the situation.

'Well, anyway, she *will* be nursing under him,' she observed with a somewhat tactless air of drawing comfort from that.

Tina bit her lip with vexation.

'I should have thought, in the circumstances,' she said, a little coolly, 'that it might be more—tasteful for Eileen to find some excuse for refusing that position. That is, if she really feels as strongly as you make out.'

'Oh, Eileen wouldn't dream of *refusing* something she really wanted. Actually, when the first shock is over, she probably won't take any notice of anything so unimportant as a mar—— Oh! Well, I didn't quite mean that, of course.' Even Audrey seemed to feel that silence might have been better than this.

'Then in that case'—Tina spoke extremely dryly—'perhaps I had better arrange that Charles withdraws that invitation for her to nurse in his convalescent home.'

This was said with a great deal more confidence than she felt. She very much doubted if she could possibly bring herself to make any objection to Charles in connection with his work. Still more did she doubt that he would take the slightest notice of her if she did.

Audrey, however, seemed to think this not a bad idea.

'It might be the best thing,' she conceded, sucking her underlip thoughtfully. 'Of course, don't, for heaven's sake, let my name appear in it anywhere! Eileen would kill me by inches if she knew I'd taken a hand. But it *would* be much better for her and all concerned if she just had to switch her plans on to someone else.'

Tina agreed, with more emphasis than she intended, that it would.

'Only don't tell him I told you about her.'

'I shouldn't dream of telling him anything you've told me,' Tina assured Audrey rather curtly. 'You would hardly expect me to discuss your sister's somewhat—extravagant feelings with him. That really would be wrong.'

'Then what excuse are you going to give for suggesting he doesn't take her on?' Audrey wanted to know.

'I don't know,' Tina confessed. 'I'll—well, I suppose I'll think of something.'

'You'll have to think pretty hard,' Audrey told her sceptically. And Tina, well aware that this was the unpalatable truth, retired to her room in a not very good temper.

Even by the time Charles came to see her, two days later, she had not thought of a tactful way to approach the Eileen problem, and decided, not very wisely, to leave it to the inspiration of the moment.

However, there were plenty of other things to be discussed.

Charles admired her ring, took it off her finger, and then put it back there personally, so that she should feel, he told her amusedly, that at least part of the usual procedure had been followed. She felt like asking him then why he could not have waited until today, so that they could have bought the ring together. But she soon found that during the short times they were able to arrange to be together there were more important things to be done than the choosing of engagement rings.

That day they went to see Mr Medway, who was delighted to find that, on emerging from the throes of obtaining probate of Aunt Maggie's will, he was immediately to engage on the buying of a house for his client.

Later, Tina and Charles drove down to the house once more, to make necessary notes and lists, and to consult with the little black-clad housekeeper.

'Consulting' was perhaps hardly the right word, for Mrs Ardingley (which it appeared was the small creature's name) seemed prepared to argue firmly over almost any arrangement which did not repeat more or less the state of things which had existed in the days of 'Sir Thomas and his lady'.

Tina was beginning to despair of their ever arranging

anything when, to her amusement, Charles firmly but quite gently took the housekeeper by the arm.

'Now look here, Mrs A. You aren't going to be able to open up this place without us, and we certainly aren't going to be able to manage without you. We've got to come to some working arrangement. I'm sure Sir Thomas and his lady had the best private house in Christendom, but that won't do for a convalescent home, you know. You don't want the place to look a poor copy of its old glory, do you? Let us have things our way, and you'll be surprised how much you like it as a new place.'

Tina guessed from Mrs Ardingley's astonished and doubtful expression that neither Sir Thomas nor his lady had ever used this method of approach. For a second she stiffened all over, in the suspicion that some affront was intended to her and her one-time employers. But one glance at Charles' vivid, coaxing smile told her that there was no question of this. Slowly her expression relaxed into the first real smile Tina had seen from her.

'Well, of course, sir, it's just as *you* say,' she told Charles primly.

And thereafter it was.

When they were driving back to London, Tina laughed and said :

'It was nice of you, Charles, to take all that trouble to win over Mrs Ardingley.'

'Was it?' He looked surprised. 'We had to make her pull in harness somehow.'

'Some people, I suppose, would have sent her away, and taken another housekeeper,' Tina said thoughtfully.

'Oh no. It would probably have killed the old lady.'

'Charles!' She smiled protestingly at what she considered a piece of picturesque exaggeration.

'I mean it. Oh, not the shock exactly. Just the fact that there was no longer anything left to live for. That house is her world. If she had to go away from it, her heart would break. Hearts do break, you know—much more often than non-medical people believe. Or, if you like it better, the spring breaks. She had to stay. We couldn't have sent her away.'

He was not sentimental about it. He was simply final. And Tina laughed and found she wanted to hug him.

'You're rather a darling, Charles.'

'Am I?' He looked amused, but not displeased, she thought, and on impulse she said:

'I hear you've already been picking your nursing staff.'

'Oh? From whom did you hear that?'

'The sister of one of your nurses. She's staying at my hotel. Audrey Unsworth is her name.'

'Oh—Nurse Unsworth?' He smiled reflectively. 'Jolly good nurse she is too.'

Tina felt unreasonably that that was the last thing she would have expected Eileen Unsworth to be.

'Is she?'

Perhaps her surprise—and something else—showed in her voice, because Charles glanced at her with raised eyebrows.

'Yes. Any reason why she shouldn't be?'

'Oh—no. I just imagined somehow that she was a bit—frivolous and self-centred.'

'She may be, outside her work.' Charles sounded indifferent. 'But what made you think so? Do you know her?'

'No. I gathered a general impression of her from her sister's attitude, and——'

'You shouldn't judge people by other people's comments,' Charles told her equably.

'I *don't*. I saw her for myself once and I thought——' Her voice trailed off, because she was not quite sure what she *had* thought, apart from the fact that she didn't like Eileen Unsworth at all.

'Oh—you mean she's so astonishingly pretty?' Charles sounded amused and unusually indulgent.

'I didn't mean that at all,' Tina retorted crisply. 'Though

of course she *is* extremely pretty,' she added, in a tone of strict fairness.

'Extremely,' Charles agreed.

And there the subject rested—very unsatisfactorily, Tina couldn't help thinking. But it was difficult to see how one could continue the argument without appearing either catty or else much more interested in Charles' professional affairs than a mere fiancée was entitled to be.

Somewhat to Tina's relief, Audrey refrained from asking her whether she had been successful in her efforts to change things, and after a while Tina told herself that the whole situation had probably been exaggerated by Audrey's highly coloured imagination. Charles probably never thought of this girl as anything but an efficient—and attractive—nurse. Any romantic feelings she had for him would surely die a natural death.

The arrangements for the convalescent home went forward without a hitch. It was as though some charm rested on the place and nothing could go wrong there.

'It's a lucky house,' Earle told Tina, when he had driven out one day to see the place, not long before the actual furnishings and fittings had been finished.

'Oh, Earle, I do hope so!'

Tina spoke with more anxiety than she knew, and Earle Morrison glanced at her with shrewd, kindly eyes.

'You sound as though that takes some believing,' he said.

'Oh, no,' Tina laughed nervously. 'I only meant—I suppose every girl marries with the idea that everything is going to be happy ever after. Only—quite often—things go wrong even then.'

'Only if the seeds are there already. Unhappiness doesn't just blow up of its own accord, you know.' Earle spoke with unusual seriousness and his drawl was more than ordinarily pronounced. 'What are you anxious about?'

'I'm not anxious,' Tina said immediately—and wished with quite passionate intensity that she could tell Earle the real state of affairs. How she was living a life of complete deception—how, in a way, she was putting that right by marrying Charles, and how, though Charles was marrying her more than half as a matter of convenience, she was finding herself more and more in love with him every time he turned his smiling, indifferent eyes on her.

But of course one couldn't tell that to anyone—not even to such an understanding person as Earle. He just had to go on thinking that everything was quite all right and that the quiet wedding—at which he himself was to be best man— would usher in a life of regulation calm and happiness for his two excellent friends.

It was by no means all the time that Tina had misgivings. Often she was much too happy enjoying the arrangement of her new home and the bright, energetic planning of her fiancé for any shadow to trouble her.

Less than a fortnight before the wedding Charles telephoned to her one morning with the urgent request that she would be free to come down with him to the house that afternoon.

'Yes, of course, if you want me.' She smiled instinctively, because Charles always sounded so boyishly excited on these occasions. 'What is the special reason?'

'Earle is bringing along one or two American fellows who want to see the place. It seems they're tremendously interested in the whole idea and want to see the lines on which we're going to work it. There'll be a couple of doctors, and I think there's a journalist among them and——'

'But you don't want a lot of press publicity, do you?'

'No, of course not. It's not that kind of stunt. I think this fellow is writing a book or something. I don't mind his seeing the place. He's a Canadian, by the way, I believe. Anyway, if he's the wrong sort, we can always turn sticky and professional and refuse to have anything written.'

'All right,' Tina laughed. 'Will you collect me here—or shall I meet you at the house?'

'Oh no! I'll fetch you. We want to be there at the same time. After all, it's a joint affair.'

He sounded quite shocked at any other notion, and Tina experienced one of those warm little rushes of happiness and relief which always came over her when Charles rather ingenuously let fall the fact that she *had* a place in his thoughts and plans.

She was ready for him when he came that afternoon, and they drove down through the autumn sunshine to the house which was fast becoming 'home' to Tina. Mrs Ardingley welcomed them with a warmth which suggested that they might even one day rival Sir Thomas and his lady in her esteem. And Tina felt that everything was well with the world.

Their visitors had not yet arrived, and she and Charles strolled round, noting one or two additions since their last visit.

'It's perfect, isn't it?' Tina drew a deep sigh of satisfaction.

'Yes, it's perfect. Just the sort of place I always longed to have.' Charles put a careless affectionate arm round her. 'Did I ever tell you that you were the dearest and most generous person in the world?'

'I, Charles?'

'Yes, of course. You always behave as though this place belongs to me——'

'Oh, but it does!' She thought of all that money which was really his and not hers. 'At least——'

'At least——?'

'Charles, can't we just think of this place as *ours*, without bothering about how we came to have it or who bought it or whether the money should have been yours or mine or half and half? It's the only way to be really happy here.'

He smiled, and she thought for a moment that he was going to tease her, but instead he bent his head and kissed her.

'All right. I don't know quite why it's so easy to accept that from you. I wouldn't take it from anyone else.'

'Perhaps,' Tina said, a little timidly, 'I'm rather different from "anyone else".'

'Perhaps,' he agreed briefly. He was obviously going to say something else when Mrs Ardingley came in to say 'the gentlemen' had arrived.

'Oh, come along then. Let's do the honours of our new home.' And Charles, still with his arm round her, took her out into the big, square, light hall.

Half a dozen people were there, and as they came forward Earle detached himself from the group and came up to them. While he greeted them, Tina glanced beyond him to the unfamiliar faces, and for an odd and disconcerting moment it seemed to her that one of the faces was *not* so unfamiliar. That man in brown, with the thin, over-keen face—surely——

But the impression was gone again, and she was listening to what Earle was saying to Charles about the eagerness of all their visitors to see the place, and to hear all that there was to hear about it.

Charles turned to the group with that smile of easy friendliness, and began to say something about how pleased he and his fiancée were to welcome them. But as he did so, the man in brown seemed to see Tina for the first time, and exclaimed:

'Why, Miss Fenwick, what are *you* doing all these miles away from N'York? The last time I saw you you were fiddling very charmingly in my brother Louis's club, not fifty yards from Fifth Avenue.'

The blow was so sudden and so utterly unexpected that Tina could think of nothing at all to say. She supposed she gazed at Louis's brother in fascinated horror, and it was left to Earle to say, quite pleasantly:

'No, there's a mistake there, I think. The lady's name——'

'Mistake?' The other man laughed. 'Oh no, I couldn't be mistaken about that. You remember me, don't you, Miss Fenwick? I remember you very well. You and that little blonde friend of yours. Now, let me see, what was her name? I'll remember it in a minute——'

He would, too. Tina could see that. She wondered wildly

if it were any good pretending to faint. But even as the idiotic idea crossed her mind, Charles spoke coolly and finally.

'My fiancée's name is Miss Frayne—Sonia Frayne. So you see, there must be a mistake.'

'Sonia Frayne,' repeated Louis's brother slowly, and Tina thought she had never heard anything so disagreeable as the note of recognition and understanding in his tone.

Somehow she recovered her own voice then and spoke, though a little breathlessly.

'Yes—you got us mixed. I remember you quite well now, Mr Collier. It was my friend who was Miss Fenwick. You— you got us mixed.'

'Sure,' he said, still speaking slowly. 'I got you mixed. Isn't that odd, now? Two such dissimilar names—and I got you mixed. You must forgive me. I thought I never forgot a face—or a name.'

'It doesn't matter.' She believed that she smiled faintly. 'I'm—very glad to meet you again, anyway.'

And then other introductions were being made, and she was trying to smile again and to make light conversation, and not to realise that everywhere she went, those light, penetrating eyes—so reminiscent of Louis—followed her with a speculative expression.

He was not in the least deceived, of course! However well the scene had passed off, and however credulous the others might be, *he* knew she was masquerading as some-one else. And if he were anything like Louis, he would never rest until he knew the reason why.

Besides—she remembered very well now—she and Sonia had put him in his place pretty thoroughly, the one other time she had seen him. He probably bore resentment for that. He was what Sonia had called 'a nasty piece of work', and they had dealt with him summarily. They were used to holding their own with that type, and the fact that he was Louis's brother had not made any difference. To tell the truth, Louis would have supported them, rather than his brother, in an argument, because however difficult he might be to work for, he never tolerated any pestering of 'his girls'.

It seemed to Tina that they trailed endlessly round, explaining things which had become meaningless and listening to admiration of things which had lost their savour.

Philip Collier made no further attempt to engage her in conversation, and any questions he asked were addressed to Charles or to Earle. She saw perfectly well that Charles disliked him, and felt pretty sure that he would refuse to have his beloved project 'written up' by someone he considered vulgar and unpleasant. Which would probably make Collier even more ready to find out unwelcome truths—and exploit them.

For a moment, while Earle was talking, Charles dropped behind and took Tina lightly by the arm.

'What is it, my dear? Are we tiring you?'

'No! Oh no.' She was alarmed that her troubled thoughts were so obvious. 'I'm *quite* all right.'

He gave her a puzzled, searching glance, as though he hardly heard her protest.

'Hm, I don't like our Canadian friend either,' was his comment. 'But don't worry. He doesn't mean a thing in your life now.'

'Oh, Charles!' She laughed a little uncertainly and squeezed his arm gratefully, because she saw that he thought she associated some unpleasant memory with Philip Collier, and he was anxious to reassure her. 'Thank you, darling.'

She had never called him anything like that before, but he didn't seem to mind. He smiled at her brilliantly and said:

'No one's going to trouble you, now you've got an able-bodied husband to look after you.'

And she thought: 'He sees himself already as my husband,' and realised how happy she would have been if this terrible shadow had not turned up out of the past.

Charles had turned away again now, to answer a query from the senior member of the party—a charming, elderly man, whose perfect manners and slightly deprecating air concealed the fact that he was a very famous surgeon indeed.

'Oh no, Mr Mason,' Tina heard Charles say, 'this isn't a Government-sponsored scheme at all. It's all rather in the experimental stage at the moment, you know. We should probably have to prove ourselves pretty thoroughly before there were any question of Government support, or anything of the kind.'

'Remarkable, remarkable,' murmured Mr Mason.

'Then is this place financed entirely by voluntary subscriptions?' inquired one of the others interestedly.

'Entirely,' Charles agreed with a laugh. 'In fact, the whole cost of the place was subscribed by my fiancée.'

There were several polite murmurs of 'Really,' and everyone turned an approving smile on Tina.

'Miss—Frayne financed the whole thing? My word, that *is* a news story,' observed Philip Collier with an emphasis which was so admiring that it was hard to take exception to it.

'Oh, I don't think she wants any publicity about it.' Charles seemed smilingly inclined to dismiss that. But Collier insisted.

'But you can't let a story like that just go dead on your hands. Do tell us, Miss—Frayne, what first gave you the idea? Were you always interested in this type of surgery— or what started you?'

Tina felt so sick and faint that she thought it must surely show in her face, but somehow she found her voice to reply:

'Well, I—didn't know much about it until I met my fiancé. And then—well, he was so much interested, you see, and—and he'd always wanted a place like this——'

Her voice trailed away. She knew Collier was consumed with curiosity to know how on earth an impecunious little musician came to have enough money for a scheme like this.

Then Earle's voice broke in—pleasant and positive:

'I don't think Miss Frayne's generosity should go without a little further explanation. She landed here expecting to claim a small legacy, and when it came to the point, the amount was a great deal more than she expected. Instead of launching out on personal spending, as most people would, she put her money into this place. I think that takes a lot of beating, for sheer unselfish generosity.'

'Remarkably generous, Miss Frayne. A really humanitarian action, if I may say so.' Mr Mason shook her by the hand, while the others nodded or smiled their approval. All except Philip Collier, who looked at her very thoughtfully, with his eyes slightly narrowed.

He knew now, of course. Or he thought he knew. He believed that she had deliberately contrived to cheat her friend of her inheritance.

Mrs Ardingley brought in tea then, and the conversation became more general.

It seemed that most of their visitors were on fairly short visits to England and were expecting to go back in a week or so. Tina strained her attention to see if she could catch anything of Collier's plans—any hint that this fearful menace would be withdrawn soon. But he offered no comment, and finally, driven by her frantic anxiety, she boldly put the question:

'And you, Mr Collier? Are you staying here long, or do you have to be back in your own country soon?'

'I, Miss—Frayne?' He never failed, she noticed, to make that slight hesitation before the name which was not hers. 'Oh, I'm rather a rolling stone, you know. No settled plans at the moment. I was thinking of going back soon—but I don't know. If I—got on to a good thing, for instance, I should probably stay a while longer.'

'I see.'

She hoped he didn't guess how dry her mouth had gone. A good thing, indeed! What did he mean by that? she thought. And she wondered if it were melodramatic of her to allow the sinister thought of blackmail to hover in the back of her mind.

After tea, as a completion to their tour, the party strolled round the really beautiful grounds, and here at last Tina's most unwelcome visitor found an opportunity to speak to her alone.

'No—don't hurry on,' his voice said quietly beside her, when she would have hastily joined the others again. 'We want a little talk, you and I.'

'You're mistaken, I think,' Tina retorted crisply. 'We don't want to talk, even if you do.'

'Is it possible that I'm mistaken again?' He laughed, but not very nicely. 'My second bad mistake this afternoon, eh?'

She was silent, but she had instinctively slackened her step to suit his.

'That's better, Miss—Frayne.' And then, as she said nothing: 'Well, well, times have changed since I saw you last. Who would have expected you to exchange a N'York club for an English country estate? I'll say you're a lucky girl.'

'I think so,' she agreed, as coolly as possible.

'Damned lucky,' he repeated reflectively. 'Lucky not to be found out, too.'

'I don't know what you're talking about.' Tina was surprised that she was able to make that so cold and haughty.

'Oh, you don't need to do that with me.' He laughed again in that unpleasant way. 'The others can call you Sonia Frayne till the cows come home, but the one thing I should like to know is—where is Sonia Frayne? If she's alive, how comes it you're able to play this little game? If she's not alive—*where and how did she die?*'

CHAPTER NINE

NOT until that moment, Tina felt, had she known the real meaning of panic.

Scared, nervous, anxious—she had been all of those at one time or another during the fantastic weeks since she had taken Sonia's passport from the drawer in the Brooklyn apartment. But at the cool, menacing note in Philip Collier's tone she felt a constriction of her throat, a sudden breathlessness, a mad desire to run away. Somewhere—anywhere—so long as there was no more need to face that bright, suspicious stare or listen to that faintly sneering voice which said such terrifying things.

With a frightful effort she controlled her impulse for flight, and faced him determinedly.

'How dare you say such a thing to me!'

She was surprised to find that her voice had grown slightly shrill.

'Such a thing as what?' He was perfectly cool.

'Implying that I—implying——' Her voice died in her throat.

'I'm not implying a thing,' he assured her smoothly. 'I'm only saying I'd like to know what happened to Sonia Frayne. She struck me as a little lady with a great talent for knowing where there was any money she could lay her hands on. I can't quite see her resigning a fortune to someone else out of pure friendship.'

Tina knew that further insistence was useless, yet she spoke with dull desperation:

'I tell you, *I* am Sonia Fr——'

'Can it,' he said with an abrupt contempt that was even

ruder than the words. 'Don't you know when you're beaten? You've done something that means a stretch in gaol if you're caught—or maybe something worse—and all you can do is repeat one silly lie, like a frightened parrot.'

They had long ago dropped behind the others, and she stopped to face him now, her lips dry and slightly parted with the terror of one thing he had said.

'What do you mean?' Her voice ran up uncontrollably again. 'What do you mean by "maybe something worse"?'

He shrugged, and gave that smile which was so much more disquieting than any other smile she had ever seen.

'Depends on what really did happen to Sonia Frayne.'

There was a heavy silence, because there was nothing Tina could think of to say.

'She's dead, isn't she?' The hateful, sneering voice was almost persuasive, as though he were trying to make her speak.

'Yes,' Tina said dully, 'she's dead.'

What was the use of struggling for further concealment?

'When?—and how?'

'You have no right——'

'When—and how? Or shall I talk the matter over with the solicitor in charge of—her legacy?'

'You don't know who he is!' Panic pricked her into life again. 'I won't tell——'

'One can always find these things out. No one is easier to trace than a solicitor, you know.'

She made a little gesture of defeat.

'She was killed—in a plane crash.' The words came jerkily. 'In the summer—some weeks before I came here. The plane crashed and then was burnt out.'

'All evidence lost, in fact?' His eyes never left her face.

'Yes.' And then as she saw his expression, 'Well, why not? Is there anything wrong with that?'

'Nothing. Except that it disposes of any support to your statements.'

'Is there any necessity for support?' Again anger swept

aside some of her fear. 'People *are* sometimes killed in accidents.'

'They are also occasionally killed *not* by accident, Miss Fenwick. Particularly when a large sum of money is involved.'

Tina gave a furious little laugh.

'Are you making the preposterous suggestion that *I* had anything to do with——'

'I'm not making any suggestion, my dear. I've told you that already. I'm just wondering how the whole story—unsupported—would sound to Sonia Frayne's relations, or solicitor—or a suspicious jury, come to that.'

'A—jury! What are you talking about? A jury!'

He shrugged again, insolently.

'Usual form of trial when someone has—disappeared in suspicious circumstances.'

'You're mad!' Tina exclaimed.

But she wondered if it were not she instead who was mad, because nothing seemed to have any coherence and meaning any more. The beautiful garden—in which she had already begun to take such pride and pleasure—seemed to become unreal around her. In the distance, at the end of the centre path, she saw Charles come into view again, explaining something to Earle and their visitors. But they too seemed unreal, like figures in a dream—or a nightmare.

Only this terrible man, with his incredible hints and the spell which his very words seemed to weave around her, was quite real. Deadly real. Much more real than anything that had happened since Sonia was killed and she had taken on Sonia's identity.

'You see,' Philip Collier said softly beside her, 'we *shall* need to have a little talk, you and I.'

She hardly knew what she would have answered, only at that precise moment Charles waved to her to come and join them, and as though indeed released from a nightmare, she started forward down the path. She would have run but for the fact that her legs seemed disinclined to obey her.

But Collier easily kept pace with her.

'Where can I find you in town?' he asked coolly, still with that touch of insolence.

'I absolutely refuse to see you again.' At the thought of her nearness to Charles, she suddenly found a little courage and reassurance once more. 'You have no concern whatever with my private affairs, and you can exercise your impudent curiosity in some other direction.'

'For instance, with the solicitor who's handling the legacy?'

Her footsteps slowed as though something had grasped her round the ankle.

'You couldn't——'

'I could. We're going to talk this thing right out, my dear. Where can I find you in town?'

They were nearly up with the others now, and it was in a desperate little undertone that she murmured the name of her hotel. He seemed to hear quite well, however, because he actually took out a small notebook and coolly made a note of it.

'I thought we'd lost you two,' Charles said casually.

'No. We—we were discussing the planning of the garden—how we mean to turn part of it into a fruit and vegetable plot,' Tina explained, with a glibness which surprised herself. 'Mr Collier is very much interested in gardens.'

'Sure.' Philip grinned with an amusement which the occasion hardly seemed to justify. 'I was always interested in—gardens.'

Charles' eyes were suddenly very bright and cold.

'That's fine.' His even tone left Collier's insolence in the shade. 'But I'm sorry I can't give you permission to write up anything about the place. We've decided to have no publicity at this stage. You'll understand, of course. I hope you won't feel your afternoon was wasted, but—there it is.'

'No,' Collier said slowly, 'I don't feel the afternoon was wasted.' And that was all he said.

Very soon after that the party left, and Tina was not sure

whether she was relieved to see the back of Collier or alarmed in case Charles should make inquiries about him.

Characteristically Charles did mention him, and went straight to the point.

'Poisonous fellow, that journalist. I suppose he made a pest of himself when you were playing in that nightclub.'

'Rather—yes. Though I only saw him once or twice, really.'

'Yes, I gathered that from his getting you mixed up with your friend. Did he corner you just now?'

'*Corner* me?'

'You needn't look so startled.' He seemed rather astonished by the expression on her face. 'I only meant—I suppose it was he who manoeuvred so that you got separated from the rest of us.'

'Oh——' She could have fainted with relief—and also with the fear that she had nearly betrayed herself. 'Oh—yes, of course. I didn't realise what you—— It was such an odd expression to use.'

'Was it?' He smiled and passed his arm round her, as he had earlier in the afternoon. 'He didn't actually make himself objectionable, did he? I would have interfered before if I'd realised——'

'No—oh no.' She hastily reassured him, because she longed for nothing so much as to have the whole subject dismissed. 'I don't like his manner, of course—and I can't say I was pleased to see him turn up here. But—but it's over now. Don't think anything more about it, Charles. I—I shan't.'

'Sure?' He turned up her face, rather abruptly she couldn't help thinking, and gave her a worried glance.

'*Quite* sure.' She somehow managed to smile at him, and he seemed satisfied for the moment.

It was not until much later that night, when she was alone in her bedroom, that she was able to face her terrible situation coolly and try to think collectedly of some way of escape. Not that cool, collected thought came naturally to her at that moment. She wandered about the bedroom, picking up things for no reason whatever and putting them down again where they didn't belong.

Of course he was not the slightest bit interested in the rights or wrongs of the case. It mattered less than nothing to him whether Tina or Sonia received the fortune involved. That meant that his interest could only arise from something which he expected to turn to his own advantage.

Again the ugly word 'blackmail' seemed to loom very near. It couldn't mean anything else but that he meant to make her pay over some big sum as the price of his silence. Oh, it would all be carefully wrapped up and called something else, of course, but that was the real meaning of his insistence on the 'little talk'.

Until that moment Tina had always had a certain surprised scorn for those people who allowed themselves to be bled of their money in order to hide some guilty secret. Now she saw their point of view with a new and dreadful sympathy.

After all, if Collier would only promise silence and *go*, it would be worth almost any sum. She had never been rich before. She could do without anything very lavish now. So long as there was enough money to start the nursing-home on a successful basis, that beast of a man could have anything—anything, she felt.

Only, she knew that the whole technique of blackmailers involved a continuance of their demands. If this man went back to Canada, there was some hope of freedom. If not——

Tina flung herself face downwards across her bed.

If only she could tell Charles! But she couldn't, of course. If she told him, she must face losing him, for even if he didn't exactly take it upon himself to upbraid her for cheating him personally, he certainly would have no use for a penniless swindler. And a clumsy one at that! With the faintest, miserable smile, Tina acknowledged that there was that element about it too. She hadn't even managed to be a successful criminal!

She spent the next few days in a fever of nervous anticipation. She longed yet dreaded to hear from Collier, feeling that until the whole situation was clear in black and white, she could not have a moment's rest, yet knowing that even this dread uncertainty might be better than the full realisation of his grim intentions.

It was hard to remember sometimes that she was to be married so soon, and that, as a happy bride, she ought not to have any greater worry than a natural anxiety that everything should go well on her wedding-day. More than once she wondered if she ought to contrive to postpone the ceremony. After all, if everything else failed and Collier did betray her to Charles, through sheer spite, it was unthinkable that she should have added to her offence by marrying the victim of her cheating.

At this point poor Tina's head always began to swim, and she wondered unhappily if she were the greatest criminal alive. And then she would remind herself ruthlessly that the only straightforward and right thing to do was to confess to Charles.

'But I can't lose him!' she thought despairingly. 'He may not love me—but I love him. And I could make him happy. I know I could make him happy, if I could only have the chance. I won't throw it all away now. I'll buy off Collier if it costs everything I have. But I *will* have my chance of happiness with Charles.'

She realised that, somehow or other, she must be managing to hide her anxieties well, because no one seemed to notice anything wrong with her. Not Charles himself—and he was usually observant enough—nor Earle, nor even the insatiably inquisitive Audrey.

'I suppose you're feeling most frightfully excited by now,' Audrey said, having managed to corner her in the hotel lounge one afternoon. 'It's only a few days, isn't it?'

'Yes,' Tina agreed. And then, feeling that needed some amplifying, 'Yes, of course I'm excited.'

But she really just felt miserable and nervous.

'You're not going out right away, are you?'

'No,' Tina admitted cautiously. 'Not right away. Why?'

'Because Eileen's coming this afternoon, and I do want you to meet her at last.'

'Oh yes, I see. I should like that,' Tina said, quite untruthfully. Though, as a matter of fact, Eileen had become a very minor worry in comparison with the much greater one of Philip Collier.

'Yes, she wants to meet you too,' Audrey explained.

Tina felt inclined to ask 'Why?' since Eileen's feelings towards her had never been depicted as particularly friendly, but she suppressed the ungracious question.

'She says,' Audrey went on, requiring no questions to make her amplify her statements, 'that it's absurd to think she hasn't met you yet, when you'll be living in the same house.'

'I shall be in our own wing of the house most of the time,' Tina retorted firmly, hoping that didn't sound too much of a snub, but feeling sure now that Eileen's desire to meet her was simply prompted by a curiosity to size up someone she regarded either as an enemy or at least as a rival.

Not that Eileen didn't make herself perfectly charming to Tina when they eventually met. But to Audrey her air of barely suppressed impatience seemed perpetually to suggest that she thought her young sister a fool and that, for her part, she was not one to suffer fools gladly.

Tina felt an indignation which surprised her. Audrey could be trying, of course, but her abundant goodwill and her puppyish desire to please and to enjoy herself on rather little were deserving of something more than this chilling treatment.

'Your sister has been very kind to me,' she told Eileen with slightly more emphasis than she intended. 'She was very friendly and made me feel at home almost as soon as I arrived here.'

Audrey looked gratified and surprised, but Eileen laughed a little slightingly.

'Oh, Audrey makes friends *very* easily,' she explained disparagingly.

'I can quite believe it. A very useful gift, don't you think?'

Eileen obviously didn't.

'Oh, I don't know,' she murmured. 'One would like a *little* discrimination shown.'

'Meaning that Audrey didn't display much in making friends with me?' asked Tina amusedly, and had the satisfaction of seeing Eileen colour.

'No, no, of course I didn't mean it that way.' The assurance was given smilingly, but Tina could see that Eileen was considerably annoyed at having her real feelings indicated—even apparently in joke. 'But Audrey hasn't much—discretion.'

'We-ell, had we at that age?' Tina inquired tolerantly, and was amusedly sure that she had thereby set Eileen guessing at just how their ages compared.

Eileen soon abandoned the subject of Audrey, however, in favour of the more interesting one of herself and her future.

'I'm looking forward so much to working in Mr Linton's nursing-home,' she said. 'He's a wonderful man to work for, you know.' Either intentionally or otherwise she made that sound as though Tina stood right outside anything so important as work.

'I'm sure he is.' Tina kept that determinedly good-tempered. 'He tells me you're a very good nurse.'

'Oh, well, it's perfectly easy to be a good nurse on his cases. At least, *I* find it so. I suppose we have something the same outlook.'

Tina supposed they had nothing of the sort, but hardly saw how she could say so.

'Or else it's a sort of—what shall I say?—sympathy between temperaments. We always seemed to work as well together from the very beginning.'

'That must be very satisfactory,' Tina said coldly, wishing that Charles, who was due to fetch her some time in the next hour, would hurry up and make his appearance, or else that Audrey—who seemed to lose her usual loquacity entirely in her sister's presence—would take harmless charge of the conversation once more.

'Are you interested at all in hospital work?' Eileen asked, but very much as though she thought Tina too frivolous to care about anything which occupied the serious side of her fiancé's thoughts.

'I've never done any nursing, if you mean that,' Tina explained crisply. 'But——'

'Oh no, I remember now. Mr Linton said that music was your chief interest.' With the slight but skilful emphasis on the word 'music', Eileen managed to imply that, incredible though it seemed, there were still people concerning themselves with trifles while people like herself and Charles Linton got on with the real work of the world.

'How dare Charles discuss me with this minx!' was the first—and furious—thought which sprang into Tina's mind. But it was banished the next moment by the voice of Charles himself speaking behind them—and as he did so, three heads turned simultaneously, as though jerked on a string.

'I can't imagine that I ever made such an assertion.' He was standing there regarding them with smiling coolness. 'I naturally assume that I am my fiancée's chief interest— and should be exceedingly disconcerted to find myself wrong.'

Eileen, Tina saw, was considerably taken aback, though she made an admirable recovery and smiled at him with a warmth and interest which she had certainly not wasted on her young sister or Tina.

'I didn't see you come in, Charles, though I thought I kept an eye on the entrance.'

'I came in by the side entrance,' he explained, and something about that seemed to amuse him.

Tina hoped it was not petty of her to wonder with some satisfaction whether Eileen were trying to recall just how candid she had been, and just how much of the conversation Charles was likely to have overheard. Audrey's open countenance displayed all too obviously that this was just what *she* was thinking.

'I was telling Miss Frayne how much I'm looking forward to working in your nursing-home,' Eileen explained quickly, perhaps to forestall any unfortunate conversational blunder on Audrey's part.

'In her nursing-home,' Charles corrected, quite charmingly but firmly.

'Oh, but I thought——'

'I'm quite sure you did. But the home was suggested, financed, and largely arranged by my fiancée. And I can't imagine'—he put his arm round Tina in that careless way of his—'that anyone of her temperament won't eventually take a good part in helping with some of the psychologically difficult cases.'

To Tina's surprise, Eileen turned a sweet and enthusiastic smile on her.

'But how splendid! I *do* think it's marvellous of you to feel like that about it.'

'Like what?' thought Tina ungraciously. But aloud she said, 'Of course I shall be terribly happy if I can help at all,' and she pressed Charles' arm a little nervously against her. She felt more disconcerted by Eileen's approval than by her disparagement. There was so little doubt that it was put on for Charles' benefit only.

There was a short silence after the two girls had gone. Then Charles said:

'That was the first time you had met Nurse Unsworth, wasn't it?'

'Yes. I knew the younger sister quite well already.'

'I remember. How do you like her?'

'The sister?'

'No, no. The elder one.'

Tina resisted a prompt desire to say that she found her detestable. She felt that here was the opportunity to say something, if any protest against her employment at the nursing-home were ever to be made. But with so little obvious grounds for objection, how was one to do it without sounding catty?

'She's extremely pretty, of course.'

'But——?'

Tina laughed and flushed slightly.

'I should say she could make trouble.'

'Of what sort?'

'Well, what sort do you think, Charles? The usual sort, of course. On the staff of a big hospital she might be quite harmless. But with a much smaller staff—in a nursing-home——' Tina broke off. Then she said: 'I think she has some idea that she's going to be of special importance in the nursing-home.'

'Nonsense!' Charles looked annoyed. 'She wouldn't be such a fool. She must know quite well that only one woman will have any special importance there.'

'The matron?' Tina suggested, quite sincerely.

'The *matron*!' Charles laughed and flushed unexpectedly in his turn. 'No—you, of course.'

He thrust his hands deep into his pockets, and she thought he was faintly surprised himself to find that he had said that.

'Oh, Charles'—she was at least as much surprised as he —'how nice of you—and how unexpected.' She smiled a little doubtfully.

'Good lord, it's not specially *nice* to tell one's fiancée that, surely. And come here and tell me why on earth it should be unexpected.' He sat down on the settee and drew her down beside him.

'Well'—she was rather at a loss to put what she meant into words, but he prompted her with an imperious 'Yes?'

'I was thinking just how we went into this. The—the rather unromantic kind of proposal you made to me——'

'Have I got to be haunted by that damned proposal for the rest of my days?' he exclaimed with impatience. 'Isn't it a bit'—he groped for the right word with less than his usual assurance—'a bit out of date in our—relationship?'

'Is it?' She turned to him with an eagerness she could

not hide. And at that moment a polite hotel porter, unaware that never in his life had he been less welcome, came up to her and said:

'You're wanted on the telephone, madam.'

'The telephone?' For a moment Tina looked as though she had never heard of such an instrument.

'Yes, madam. A Mr Collier, I think the name was.'

CHAPTER TEN

WITH the suddenness of an electric shock, the man's respectful announcement jerked Tina back from happy security to an acute realisation of her real position.

'Mr Collier?' she repeated stupidly. And then, 'Oh yes, of course—Mr Collier.'

The man withdrew, and Tina, with an effort that made her physically tired, made to stand up. But Charles held her back for a moment with a puzzled smile.

'Why "of course"?' he wanted to know. 'I thought we'd seen and heard the last of that man.'

'So did I.' She somehow managed to smile faintly. 'But I suppose there's something he wants to know. I said "of course" because—because—well, I couldn't place the name at first, and then I remembered. I shan't be a moment, Charles.' She was on her feet now and managing to smile down at him quite naturally.

'How about my taking the call for you?' He grinned up at her lazily. 'Wouldn't that be the best way?'

'Oh no. No—really, Charles, it's all right. I expect it's some— some trifle. I shan't be long,' she repeated a little feverishly now, and he nodded casually. If he noticed anything wrong he made no sign of the fact.

She hurried to the telephone-box, though there was a leaden sensation about her feet that made it difficult to move quickly. And even when she had shut the door of the box behind her, she felt that there was something terribly public about all this—that someone must see her through the glass panel and be able to detect from her expression that she was agitated beyond measure.

'Yes?' She spoke rather sharply into the instrument. 'This is Miss Frayne speaking.'

'Who?' drawled the unpleasant, familiar voice the other end. 'Oh—Miss Frayne. My little friend Miss Frayne, eh? Collier speaking.'

'So I gathered.' She made that as aloof and indifferent as possible. But when a slight silence succeeded her remark, anxiety forced her to take the initiative with an urgent, 'Well, what do you want?'

'How did you know I *wanted* something? That was clever of you. As a matter of fact, I'm in rather a jam and I wondered if you could help me—for the sake of old times, you know.'

Anything less like the tone of a man really asking a favour could hardly have been imagined, and Tina guessed, with a cold, unpleasant sensation, that the degree of his offensive familiarity was an indication of his belief in his power over her.

'What is it you want me to do?' She spoke coldly, but in a tone that did not preclude further conversation. At any rate it seemed to satisfy him, because he laughed slightly.

'It's rather embarrassing——' He didn't sound in the least embarrassed. 'A question of money——'

There was a long silence. Then he said:

'Are you still there?'

'Yes,' Tina said dully, 'I'm still here.'

She could hardly believe that the moment had really come, that the demand of a blackmailer was being conveyed to her in smooth and faintly menacing tones over the telephone. She knew that the very essence of dealing with this sort of thing was to be firm from the first. And yet——

'How much do you need?' she heard herself saying.

'Why, that's awfully nice of you. Not even to ask about the circumstances, I mean.'

'The circumstances don't interest me,' Tina said curtly.

'No? Well, I feel bound to explain to you that I've been expecting a cheque from Canada and it hasn't come. Very inconvenient, you know, when one is so far from home.

And I started casting round in my mind as to who there was I could ask to—accommodate me for the moment. And I thought, "Why, Miss Frayne, of course! She's been so—lucky herself. She's bound to sympathise with someone who's out of luck." '

'Is this,' asked Tina dryly, 'the "little talk" to which you referred the other day?'

But he was evidently not going to allow any pulling of the chain.

'God bless my soul, no, my dear! We shouldn't have that over the telephone, you know. You've got such a lot to tell me. No, I'm afraid we'll have to postpone that.' Her heart leapt with hope. But his next words dashed any sanguine thoughts. 'I have to go up North on a story. I may not be back for a week or two, but I'll look you up at the nursing-home when I do come back. You'll be Mrs Linton by then, won't you?'

She knew what that pleasant-toned inquiry meant. That he realised perfectly well she would have even more to lose by the time he really put the screw on.

'How much do you want?' she repeated abruptly, without replying to his other question.

'Oh, I think a hundred would see me through nicely,' he told her casually.

A hundred? The impertinence of it! If she agreed to this demand, which was preposterous as a loan from a casual acquaintance, then she tacitly admitted that he had the grounds for blackmailing her. She would be admitting fear, and doubling his power. He had arranged it all with superb cunning.

And yet if she *didn't* agree——

'I suppose you don't want it as a cheque?' she said.

'No, no.' He laughed. 'Cheques can be terribly incon-venient things. Cash—not too large amounts. And you might meet me with it tomorrow at King's Cross. I'm catching the two-fifteen. Be there at two—near the de-parture indicator.'

The cool effrontery with which he gave his orders nearly

made her smash down the receiver there and then. Instead she said between tight lips:

'I'll be there.'

'Good girl!'

Tina felt in that moment that she hated him almost more for his insolence than the danger he represented. But she was powerless to exercise either anger or hate.

'Is that all?' she asked curtly.

'Yes, that's all.'

She thought he added some laughing remark to that, but she didn't wait to hear it, and she was ringing off before he had completed his sentence.

And now she must go back and face Charles, with her mind in a whirl and her head aching with the strain of fear and anger that had been put upon her. He would be sure to ask some question about the call—and what was she to say?

No inspiration came to her as she made her way slowly back. And it was not until Charles' casual, 'Well, what did our Canadian want?' gave nervous stimulation to her invention that she felt something click into place, and heard herself answering quite calmly:

'Oh, he was stuck for the address of someone he wanted to get in touch with in the States. He thought I might know it. Someone who used to come to the club quite a lot.'

'And could you give it to him?'

'No,' she said coolly, 'I didn't know it.'

'I'm glad.' He grinned at her.

'Are you?' she said in some surprise. 'Why?'

'Because I should hate to think you were able to oblige him in any way,' Charles told her.

'Oh!' She managed to laugh at that. But she wondered what Charles would have said if he had known in what way she was going to have to oblige Philip Collier. 'He doesn't matter, in any case,' she said, with an impatient sigh.

'Yes, he does.' Charles got up from the settee where he had still been lounging. 'He's taken nearly all the time I had, confound the fellow!—he and those stupid girls be-

tween them. My dear, I only had about half an hour. I
meant to tell you before, but we were talking of something
else.'

Something else! Yes, indeed they had been talking of
something else. And now, thanks to Collier, the magic
moment had gone. One couldn't go back to a discussion
like that. It only came—unexpectedly and of its own accord
—on rare occasions. If that thrice-cursed telephone call had
not come just when it did, Charles might have said so much
—so much—of the way their relationship had changed. He
had been going to. He had meant to put something into
words which had not been said between them before. Now
it might never be said. Because, with the ever-present
menace of Collier not far away, life *could* crash at any
moment.

Charles was reaching for his coat, which he had flung
over the back of a chair, and now he was shrugging himself into it, talking to her all the time—absolutely unaware
that she was still wondering desperately if there were any
way of recapturing the moment that had fled.

'Can you manage dinner tomorrow, Sonia?' (How she
hated that name—particularly from him!) 'Lateish. Say
quarter-past eight. Earle wants us both to join him then if
we can. I can manage it, so long as neither of you mind
waiting until then.'

'I don't mind.' She had recovered entirely now, and
smiled at him. 'I'd like to see Earle. Where does he want us
to meet?'

He named a nearby hotel. 'If you get there about eight,
I'll be along the first moment I can.' He bent his head to
give her a hasty—and perhaps rather perfunctory—kiss. He
was himself again—busy, good-tempered, but without
much time for the purely romantic.

She let him go, with a casual little kiss in her turn. No
need to embarrass them both by a display of feeling he
was not willing to second.

When he had gone she went slowly to her room.

The idea had come to her once again—as it had in the

early days—that perhaps the only (though desperate) solution to the whole problem was for her to slip away, and try to arrange that none of the actors in this drama should ever see her again.

She would have to leave some sort of explanation for Charles, of course—one of those silly notes of explanation that the heroines of fiction always seemed to leave behind them.

But how much could she explain—and how much leave untold? And what would Charles' position be then? Suppose it created some dispute about his title to the money? That would mean the end of his cherished nursing-home idea, and he would find himself personally responsible for a great deal of expense which had already been incurred.

A restless and unhappy night did nothing to help her make up her mind, and she went to her rendezvous with Philip Collier next day with her thoughts as confused as they were unhappy.

It was unexpectedly cold, and as she was early she had the added misery of waiting about in the chilly and dreary approach to the station, before going to take up her stand by the indicator. Just as she had decided to go, someone beside her exclaimed:

'Hello, Miss Frayne! How odd that we should meet again like this.'

And, turning reluctantly, Tina found herself meeting the smiling, curious gaze of Eileen Unsworth.

There was no one in London whom she could have seen with less pleasure at that moment, but there was nothing to do about it but accept the situation with as good a grace as possible.

She returned Eileen's greeting as cordially as she could manage, and said something conventional about being surprised that she was off duty again so soon.

'Oh, but I'm having two or three days' break, you know,' Eileen explained. 'I've really finished up at the hospital and am not due to start at the nursing-home until the end of the week.'

'I see.' Then the whole thing was already arranged. It would have been useless to make any protest to Charles yesterday, even if she could have thought of one to make. She remembered now how completely they had been side-tracked from the question.

She must accept things as they were. And again Eileen seemed only a small irritant compared with the menace of Philip Collier.

But she was a rather dreadfully knowing irritant! And Tina realised with dismay that the place where she was to meet Collier was plainly visible from where she and Eileen were standing. Already she could see him approaching, looking round among the crowd as though he expected her to be punctual.

'I'm seeing someone off on the two-fifteen,' she explained quickly. 'I must go, I'm afraid.'

Eileen said goodbye immediately, but as Tina left her, she had the distinct impression that Eileen didn't turn away at once. That she watched, in fact, surreptitiously but effectually, to see whom Tina was meeting.

It was ridiculous to mind, of course. The girl was nothing more than uncharitably curious, and there was not the slightest reason in the world why she shouldn't see Tina greet some male acquaintance.

But the habit of fear, Tina had already discovered, was one that grew with dreadful rapidity. And as she came up to Philip Collier, she felt that there was danger behind as well as in front.

He grinned as soon as he set eyes on her, and Tina found herself hoping that it was not obvious to Eileen, if she were still watching, how familiar and confident that grin was.

'Good girl! You're just on time. I thought for a moment that you were going to be late, or even that you weren't coming. And that would have been just too bad—for one of us.'

Tina said nothing. There was really nothing to say. And after a moment he went on:

'Have you got that—letter you were going to have for me?'

Without a word she produced the thick envelope from her handbag, and with hardly a glance at it, he took it and thrust it into his breast-pocket. Evidently he was sure enough of his hold on her not to have any fears that she would try to cheat him.

'Well, I won't stay. My train is already in. Let me give you my good wishes on the approaching marriage and, as I said, I'll look you up some time soon—when you're Mrs Linton.'

She spoke then—coldly and on the impulse of the moment.

'There may not be a wedding—but that's hardly your business.'

She was not quite sure why she said that. Whether it was an expression of the confusion and doubt in her own mind as to what she should do, or whether it was for the sheer satisfaction of seeing something like dismay on his hated face.

'Not be a wedding? Don't be a fool,' he said roughly. 'Why shouldn't there be a wedding?'

'If I decided not to—not to involve Charles in this——' she began. But he laughed in an unpleasant but relieved way.

'Don't tell me any of that stuff. I've watched you when you're with him, and you're not going to give up your glamour-doc without a struggle, believe me! He mayn't be specially sweet on you, but there's not much you aren't prepared to do to keep him. I don't blame you, my dear. He's the kind the women always like. If you don't grab him, someone else'll be mighty pleased to get him. I bet half his nurses think they're in love with him, and some of the patients too.' And Collier laughed contemptuously.

'I think you're loathsome,' Tina said with a sort of despairing hate. But there was no real satisfaction in saying that sort of thing, of course, and it seemed to her that his mocking laughter followed her all the way out of the station.

It was impossible to go straight back to her hotel and sit in ghastly inaction while her thoughts tormented her. And it would be very little better to be seized upon by Audrey and have her thoughts distracted by trifles, while all the time the heavy weight of her unsolved problem pressed upon her mind.

Suppose she told Charles when she saw him tonight? Waited until their dinner with Earle was over, of course, and then confessed to him on the way home. Wouldn't it be worth almost anything to be free from the pressure of her growing fear of Collier?

For a moment the idea of being able to defy Collier—of not having to dread his return to London, his next telephone call, his next demand—seemed to her the most heavenly thing that could happen, and worth almost any sacrifice.

But the next moment she faced the thought that she would lose Charles. Unquestionably she would lose him. One had to love someone a very great deal to forgive the tangle of cheating of which she had been guilty. And he didn't love her a very great deal. That was the crux of the matter. He liked her, thought well of her (since he didn't know the truth), and was distinctly fond of her in a smiling, lighthearted way. But that wasn't enough. Oh, not nearly enough.

And what that odious man had said was true. There would be many other women 'mighty pleased to get him'. He wouldn't need to suffer any heartbreak over a cheap little fraud whom he had mistakenly thought charming. Now that he'd begun to think about women in the marrying sense, instead of just something amusing and charming in between periods of hard work, he would turn fairly easily to someone else.

'It's unspeakably small-minded to let a thought like that affect my decision,' thought Tina wretchedly, 'but it does—

it does! I can't bear the thought of him with someone else. With Eileen or—oh, anyone.'

And yet, if that *were* the best thing for him, perhaps one could do it. Loving a person meant wanting the best thing for them, and could she pretend that, considering everything, she was the best woman for Charles?

'I could do everything, I think, except the actual *telling*,' Tina thought with a shiver. 'How *could* I face him and see astonishment and contempt growing in his face? Besides, I've never seen Charles angry yet, and I think it—can't be very nice to do so. Especially if one is the cause of it oneself.'

She was no nearer any real decision by the time she went out that evening, but at least she had established it as a *possibility* in her own mind that she would tell Charles everything tonight.

He had not yet come when she arrived at the hotel, and as Earle came forward smilingly to greet her, she could not help thinking of that other time—not so long ago—when the rôles were reversed. When she and Charles had waited for Earle, and she had begun to get to know her so-called cousin for the first time.

Earle was in very good spirits and greeted her with:

'Hello! Well, what does it feel like to be nearly a married woman?'

'Earle, I'm not sure that sounds quite respectable,' she said with a smile. 'But it feels very nice in any case.'

'I'm glad.' He settled her comfortably on a settee in the lounge and ordered drinks for them. 'So you've decided to wash out those unkind little criticisms you used to make about friend Charles?' And he grinned at her teasingly.

'Used I to criticise him?' She sipped her gin and tonic, and relaxed for the first time that day. Earle was such soothing, good-natured company—and he had no vital part in this tragic problem of hers. One could just be comfortable with him and enjoy his nonsense.

'Criticise? Say, what do you call it when a girl accuses a man of blowing his own trumpet too much, of being a mercenary fellow, and of not being very tolerant?'

'Did I really say all that about Charles?'

'At one time or another,' Earle assured her with enjoyment.

'Well, I take it back now.' Tina smiled. 'I think——' She hesitated, and then said with a little sigh, 'I think he's a darling, and that any woman who gets him is lucky.'

'Yourself, in fact,' Earle said.

'Yes,' Tina agreed slowly, 'myself.'

There was a slight pause, and then, rather as though he sensed she needed some sort of reassurance, he said:

'Well, no one deserved the luck more, my dear. You are the ideal match for Charles.'

'*I* am? Do you think so?' She flushed slightly, extremely gratified by the remark and forgetting that surprise on her part must seem somewhat out of place.

'Why, surely!' Earle laughed. 'Did you doubt it?'

'No—not in a way, of course. That is—I think—I hope we shall be happy together. But sometimes—I don't want to sound too Victorian and doormat-ish—but sometimes I wonder if I'm—good enough for him.'

'Then don't wonder a moment longer,' Earle assured her warmly. 'I see a great difference in Charles since he knew you—and it's all to the good. A man doesn't change that particular way unless he's darned happy. And I for one think Charles has found his happiness all right.'

'Earle, you do say the nicest things.' She smiled at him. 'And sometimes you really mean them, don't you?' she added mischievously.

'Mean them? I always mean every word I say,' he declared with a grin.

'You do not. You say just the nicest things that come into your head because you simply can't help trying to make the next person feel good.'

'Sounds a bit simple-minded, put that way.'

'Oh no. It's very comforting sometimes, Earle.'

'Well, you shouldn't need comforting,' he protested. 'Not at this junction. But anyway, I meant what I said about you and Charles. It's not just my own observation, either. He said as much himself.'

'Said as much as what?' She sat up very straight suddenly, the flush much deeper this time.

'Do you really want to know?' He grinned again.

'Of course.'

'Oh, we were talking a few nights ago—the way one does very occasionally, you know,' he explained vaguely. 'And Charles said, "It's strange to find suddenly that so much of one's happiness depends upon one person."'

'He said *that*!'

'He did.'

'And he meant me?'

'We-ell, I should say so,' drawled Earle amusedly. 'Who else could he mean, I should like to know? He said also that it was a little alarming to find oneself in that state.'

'Oh—dear Charles!' She laughed. 'How silly of him!'

'Very silly, I should say,' agreed Earle comfortably. 'I should imagine his happiness would be remarkably safe in your hands.'

She didn't answer that, because she was suddenly remembering by what a slender thread her own happiness hung, and that, in view of what Earle said, Charles' happiness, too, could not be so secure.

What would it mean to him now if she insisted on telling him that she had lied and cheated and taken his money? That *was* what it amounted to, if one liked to be ruthless about it. It would be the most terrible disillusionment, the most cynical shock.

She *must* not let him know, if she could help it. She must take up the burden of her secret again and carry on somehow, even if it meant living for heaven knew how long under the menace of Philip Collier's demands.

'You know Charles very well, don't you, Earle?' she said slowly.

'I should do. I've known him for a good while, at any rate, and—yes, we've always been pretty good at understanding each other's thoughts and points of view.'

'And you think—honestly—that I'm very much the right type of girl for him?'

'I'm not talking of types,' drawled Earle, with more than usual emphasis. 'Types don't mean much to a man like Charles. It's individuals that count. And you're the one individual girl that's right for him.'

Tina smiled slightly—with sheer pleasure at his view. But she answered seriously:

'Only we said once, you know—when you and I were discussing him some time ago—that he didn't know much about falling in love, or something of the sort. That he was rather inclined to be amused by anything he had never had to take seriously.'

'That's still true.'

'Then I don't see——'

'Don't you? Hasn't it struck you that he's at any rate beginning to take you seriously?' Earle broke off and laughed a little uncomfortably. 'That sounds rather a funny thing to say to a girl who's just going to get married. Something of an understatement, I suppose. But——'

'No, no, you needn't apologise,' Tina said almost absently. 'I know he wasn't taking me specially seriously when we—when we first fixed this thing up. But if you think that now——'

'I do think,' Earle stated firmly. 'And here he is to confirm that for you himself.'

Tina glanced quickly across the lounge to where Charles was standing looking round for them.

'Don't say anything,' she pleaded quickly. 'Not even in joke, I mean.'

And Earle, who possessed that rare quality—the understanding of when a joke ceases to be a joke—nodded in a matter-of-fact manner and said:

'Sure. I've forgotten everything you said to me.'

Charles came over then, with an apology for having kept them waiting, and they all went in to dinner.

It was quite a bright meal, in spite of Tina's secret preoccupation. Earle took it as a matter of course that they were excited and happy about their approaching marriage, and Charles insensibly slipped into the rôle which Earle appeared to think natural for him in the circumstances.

To Tina there was a sort of perilous pleasure about it all. She felt a feverish excitement because of all that Earle had said, and yet the sheer joy of discovering that there was so much more to Charles' feelings for her made the thought of losing him all the more poignant.

It seemed to her that she was never again to know tranquil happiness in any form. There would always be this insecure joy, alternating with breathtaking fear.

But as she looked at Charles across the table now, she thought, 'Even that's better than losing him.'

He was a good deal relaxed at the moment, listening amusedly to some of Earle's nonsense, his handsome, slightly arrogant mouth curved in a smile and his eyes sparkling.

Even as she looked at him, his glance met hers, and quite unexpectedly he put his hand over hers as it lay on the table, and kept it there until Earle had finished what he was saying.

Then he said:

'What did you do with yourself today? Were you trousseau-buying, or don't you go in for that sort of thing?'

'Oh, Charles! Of course I do,' she protested with a smile. 'But I wasn't buying it today.'

'No?' He smiled at her with a curious touch of indulgence in his expression. Then he added as an afterthought, 'Oh no, you were in the wrong district for that, weren't you? Who were you seeing off at King's Cross this afternoon, by the way?'

CHAPTER ELEVEN

CHARLES asked his question almost idly—certainly without any suspicious intention of frightening unexpected information out of her—but she could hardly have been more scared or dismayed if he had struck her.

Only with the greatest difficulty did she conceal how agitated she was, and completely unable to think out a satisfactory reply, she parried with a rather feeble:

'Who told *you* I was at King's Cross this afternoon?'

'Nurse Unsworth did, as a matter of fact.'

'Nurse Unsworth! When did you see her?'

Tina was really only playing for time, but she saw Charles' eyebrows go up at that, and she thought distractedly: 'Oh, I'm sounding like some petty, suspicious little idiot who doesn't like her fiancé to speak to another woman.'

Presumably Charles thought somethig like that too, because his tone was distinctly dry as he said:

'Well, my dear, since you ask me, I called in at the hotel on my way along. I thought I was earlier than I actually was, and intended to pick you up. Nurse Unsworth and her sister were in the lounge, and when I asked about you, we had a few moments' conversation and she happened to mention that she saw you seeing someone off at King's Cross this afternoon.'

' "Happen" my foot!' thought Tina rudely, knowing that things only 'happened' to Eileen Unsworth just as she intended them to. But she was recalled by Charles saying softly, and with a touch of amused impatience:

'Explanation satisfactory?'

'Oh, Charles, of course!' She flushed and managed to laugh. 'I'm sorry. Did I sound——'

'A little bit,' he told her with a smile.

'What a shame!' By some extraordinary exercise of self-control she was beginning to assume an air of casual amusement herself. 'I was really thinking of something else. In fact—how odd it is that one can't see off a tiresome acquaintance even in a place the size of London without someone "happening" to see one. He was some wretched man I—I met on the plane. He was in London for a day or two and looked me up to have lunch with him today before he went back north to his own people. Rather a bore, really, only he—he'd had a good deal of bad luck since he landed. I suppose it was a sort of general sympathy that—that made me give up an odd half-hour to see him off on his train.'

There was a short silence. Then Charles said:

'Well, we seem to have disposed of Nurse Unsworth and the mysterious gentleman at King's Cross.'

'Oh, Charles, he *wasn't* mysterious!' She was unable to hide her distress. 'He was just——'

'My dear, I know.' He was surprised and contrite. 'I was only teasing you. Forget it.'

He turned immediately to say something to Earle, and Tina was left wondering feverishly if she had magnified the whole incident in such an unfortunate way that it would stick in Charles' memory very effectively.

She felt distractedly that it was impossible to go on like this. And then, after conversation had flowed quite normally again for ten minutes, she knew that it was not only quite possible to go on, but that there was literally nothing else she could do. Not after what Earle had told her.

Only the effort would sometimes be almost more than she could bear.

When Earle said goodnight to them that evening, he added:

'And I suppose the next time I see you will be when I come to play my part as witness.'

'Not until then?' Tina smiled at him, though the sudden nearness of that occasion seemed to come home to her very forcibly as he said that.

'I'm afraid not. Work's pretty heavy just lately, you know. I'm lucky to be sure of getting away for the wedding.'

'I know.' Charles made a grimace. 'I'm lucky to be almost sure of three days for my honeymoon.'

Tina hugged his arm suddenly and said:

'Then I'm lucky to have you both spending your little bit of spare time on me.'

Charles laughed and kissed her lightly.

'Nothing short of half a dozen "emergencies" shall interfere with that,' he promised her.

After that the last few days slipped away with a peculiar uneventfulness. Tina heard nothing further of Collier and saw nothing further of Eileen, since she had already gone down to the nursing-home to take up her duties there.

Audrey made her a present of her company on several occasions, but as she was cheerful, good-tempered, and undemanding, she made an engaging companion for the few shopping expeditions Tina had to make and the last-minute arrangements.

'It must feel funny to have no one of your own at a time like this,' Audrey remarked reflectively one afternoon. 'I mean, you expect a terrific gathering of the clans for anything like a wedding, and you can't even produce a second cousin or an aunt by marriage, can you?'

'No,' Tina agreed somewhat crisply. 'Not one single relation.'

She thought of the remote connections of her own parents who, mercifully, knew little of her and cared less. They had no idea that she was back in England, still less that she was going to be married. And, as things were, she couldn't see that she was ever likely to have any connection with them again. One could not indulge in inexplicable relations—however remote—if one were impersonating someone else.

Still, as Audrey said, it did seem strange to be so entirely without connections, and for a moment she felt isolated and lonely. Then she remembered that her very loneliness was her safety. And anyway, in a very short time now she would have Charles for her nearest relation—and that would be sufficient.

'I suppose,' Audrey said, 'that any relations you have are in America?'

'No.' Tina wished she were not perpetually presented with the confusion of her relations and Sonia's relations, who somehow had to be reconciled into a credible family— and then dismissed *en bloc*. 'Any close relations I had are— are all dead. And I suppose one loses sight of the remote ones.'

'I suppose so.' Audrey sucked her underlip thoughtfully. 'Even Mr Linton isn't really your relation, is he?'

'No. Just a cousin by—well, I suppose, by adoption.'

'Funny you should meet like that and just fall for each other,' Audrey remarked. 'But romantic, of course,' she added as an afterthought, and Tina rather supposed she had resigned herself to the fact that Eileen had lost him, since the circumstances were what Audrey herself chose to regard as romantic.

There was a short silence and then Audrey said:

'I don't want to say anything I *shouldn't*, but you've been nice to me, and I shouldn't like things to go wrong for you——' She paused, and Tina smilingly inquired:

'Well?'

'Only that Eileen hasn't entirely given up any thought of Mr Linton just because he's marrying you, you know.'

'But, Audrey'—Tina felt her tone of reasonable protest expressed rather more amused confidence than she really felt—'even your determined sister can hardly expect to make much—headway, shall I say?—with a newly married man.'

'There's such a thing,' Audrey pointed out obstinately, 'as making trouble between husband and wife. And—I know it sounds piggish to say it of one's own sister—Eileen isn't above doing that. You see, she has a theory that if a girl can't keep her husband or fiancé or whatever it is, she just deserves to lose him.'

'Our old friend jungle law, in fact,' murmured Tina. 'Well, I'm not altogether surprised, Audrey, but don't worry about it. I don't think she will have much opportunity of exercising her theory. Charles isn't exactly— stupid, you know.'

'No,' Audrey agreed, 'and he's very fond of you. One can see that.' ('Can one?' thought Tina, amused and gratified.) 'I only meant—be careful not to give Eileen any handle against you.'

'That is to say, if I have any dark secrets, *keep* them secret,' Tina said, hardly knowing why she put it quite like that.

'Exactly.' Audrey seemed to think the description fitted the situation admirably, and she dropped the subject after that, leaving Tina to wonder what trouble—if any—Eileen could make out of that chance glimpse of Collier.

But nothing occurred to upset the tranquillity of those last few days. And on a singularly bleak November day, Earle and Audrey Unsworth and—rather surprisingly— Mr Medway foregathered to witness Tina being married (in a false name, when one came to think of it) to Charles Linton.

'A most—ah—happy termination to your trip to Europe,' Mr Medway said affably to Tina, when he was congratulating her after the short ceremony.

'Not exactly a termination, Mr Medway. Surely a beginning?' protested Earle with a smile.

'Ah, well, in the sense only of "a happy ending".' Mr Medway insisted on making himself entirely clear. 'I remember when Mrs Linton'—he bowed to Tina in acknowledgment of her changed name—'first came to see me after her arrival in England, and I apprised her of her good fortune in the matter of her legacy, she was so much exercised on behalf of her cousin that her pleasure in the legacy was almost obscured.'

'Exercised on my behalf? Why should she be?' Charles wanted to know.

'She had the idea—and, if she will allow me to say so, it was an idea that did her heart more credit than her head —she had the idea that some injustice had been done to you, Mr Linton, by *her* inheriting the money. Now she need have no misgivings of that sort.' Mr Medway beamed upon Tina, rather as though he himself were in some way responsible for the satisfactory solution. 'The happy ending—as I have observed—is complete.'

Charles laughed, and the look he gave Tina was tender.

'Yes,' he said, 'I think even her most generous scruple can be satisfied now.'

Tina managed to smile in return, but she wished that she would not be pursued even on her wedding-day by a reference to the fraud she had practised—which, of necessity, must always appear to other people as the height of generosity!

To her surprise, she felt overwhelmingly tired by the time the party broke up, and she was thankful beyond expression when all the goodbyes had been said and the good wishes expressed.

Charles and she had a long journey before them, for they had decided that, even for three days, it was worth while going to some spot in Devonshire which he was anxious to show her.

'England is your country again now,' he had told her. 'It's time you got to know it.' And she had had to pretend a pleased curiosity on the subject of a part of the country she knew well.

She found that, in an apparently casual way, he looked after her admirably. Without being told, he seemed to sense that she was tired and suffering from a certain amount of strain. Presumably he put it down to the excitement of the wedding and the uncertainty that was bound to attend this venture on an entirely new life. At any rate, he asked no awkward questions, appeared to require no explanations, but simply saw to it that she was very comfortably ensconced in the corner of a first-class compartment.

If she had no wish to talk, she was welcome to be silent, watching the wintry light fading over the hills and fields, and thinking her own thoughts.

She glanced across at him and, meeting his eyes, smiled.

'Happy?' he wanted to know. And when she nodded he seemed quite satisfied. Charles could be curiously undemanding for such an arrogant man, she thought.

It was hard to realise that she was really his wife now. That their lives, for good or ill, were irrevocably bound together. She began to wonder—not for the first time, but with added urgency now—what Charles expected of this marriage of his. Whether, in the beginning at any rate, he rather thought they would continue their pleasant, friendly, slightly impersonal relationship, or whether there would be much more to it from the very opening of their married life.

She glanced across at him again and thought worriedly, 'I wish I knew.'

He was looking out of the window too now, and she could not gather much from his profile. He looked as though his thoughts were rather far away—perhaps with his patients instead of his wife! There was a certain firmness about his jaw which made one feel that things would be as he wished, rather than as anyone else wished, but Tina was not sure that was not corrected by the essentially sweet-tempered set of his mouth.

Charles *was* sweet-tempered, she reflected with a smile. She had never seen him really irritable or ill-natured. Earle's description of him fitted extraordinarily well—'gay and slightly outrageous'. There was something reassuring about that, even when one had just married him and was wondering, quite crudely, what was going to happen next.

Most couples, she supposed, 'had things out' beforehand. But then their engagements were probably of a very different order. All romantic impulse and intimate discussion. She could not recall that she and Charles had ever discussed anything specially intimate, and for a moment she thought in panic: 'Have I married practically a stranger?'

Then she remembered that Charles had never seemed quite a stranger to her and that, from the moment he had made his unconventional proposal, she had known that to go with him and be his wife would be the most wonderful and exciting adventure, whatever else might be involved.

She supposed afterwards that she must have fallen asleep and slept for a long time. Because when she opened her eyes again it was quite dark and all the blinds in the compartment had an air of having been drawn long ago.

Charles was reading—the strong, handsome lines of his face slightly emphasised by the light cast from the lamp immediately above his head. But whatever his book was, it could not have been commanding more than perfunctory attention, because the moment she stirred he glanced up.

'We shall be in in about a quarter of an hour now,' he told her.

'Oh, Charles, I must have slept a long time. I'm sorry,' she murmured, still rather sleepily.

'Why?' He laughed at once. 'It's the best way of passing the time on a journey.'

'Even a honeymoon journey?' objected Tina with a smile.

'A honeymoon journey isn't different from any other, except that you're with someone who wants you to do exactly as you like,' he said with an oddly deliberate air.

She didn't know quite what to say in answer to that, so she was silent, but she had an idea that he had said it with the definite intention of reassuring her.

When they finally reached the small country station he actually lifted her out—remarkably easily, she thought— and while he was reaching back into the compartment for their luggage, she stood looking round, seemingly enveloped by utter darkness.

After a few moments, however, her eyes became used to the lack of light, and she saw that there were bright, cold stars twinkling overhead and a few station lights pierced the blackness. One, moving down the platform towards them, was evidently held by the one and only porter.

He whistled the train out imperiously, and then collected their luggage, informing them that a car was waiting for them. Tina wondered amusedly how he knew the car was for them. Then she realised that they were the only passengers, which certainly did rather simplify his job.

Outside the station an extremely comfortable closed car was waiting for them, and soon they were driving through the dark country lanes in what seemed a warm, intimate little world of their own.

Charles passed his arm round her and inquired:

'All right?'

And she said, 'Oh yes, Charles,' with the sudden, delicious feeling that everything was quite all right.

Collier seemed a thousand miles away. Eileen had ceased to exist. And all those odd doubts and questionings which she had had on the journey down could somehow be left quite safely to whatever solution Charles chose.

The hotel which he had chosen was the most fascinating place Tina had ever seen. Originally a country house, built on a lavish, and even luxurious, scale, it retained all the character of a country mansion while embodying every comfort of the most up-to-date hotel.

Charles was evidently quite well known there, and was received with measured enthusiasm by one or two of the staff—almost all of whom were elderly and had the air of being family retainers of almost legendary fidelity.

'You can't see anything of the outside tonight,' Charles said, 'but tomorrow I'll take you down the valley. It runs straight down to the sea. You'll love it.'

And Tina agreed that she was perfectly sure she would.

They were shown into a big, panelled bedroom, where a great wood fire blazed in an open grate.

'Oh, how lovely!'

Without even waiting to take off her things she went over to the fire and stood there looking down into its glowing heart, her hands outspread towards the blaze. Behind her she heard Charles saying something to the servant about the luggage and then the man withdrew.

'It's the loveliest room I've ever seen.' She spoke over her shoulder to him.

'Is it?' He stood there, smiling, his hands thrust into the pockets of his overcoat, which he had not yet taken off. 'I thought you'd like it. It's the room I always had when I used to come down here years ago.'

'I hope you don't mind sharing it then, if you're used to having it to yourself.' She smiled down into the fire.

There was a little silence. Then he came over slowly and put his arms round her from behind.

'Do you want me to share this room with you?' He kissed the side of her cheek lightly.

'Why, Charles!' She turned her head and gave him a startled little glance. 'I thought—— Didn't you mean to share it with me?'

'There is another room for me next door if you don't want me here,' he said coolly, but he didn't meet her eyes.

'But, my dear——' She turned in the circle of his arms, so that she was close against him. 'Don't you want—I mean, do you *prefer* to be alone?'

He smiled slightly.

'I told you—you've come on this honeymoon with some-one who wants you to do exactly as you like.'

'Even to that extent, Charles?' she said slowly.

'Even to that extent.'

She was silent for a moment, trying to decide what complicated—or perhaps perfectly simple—feeling had prompted that offer. Then, suddenly, on an instinct much deeper than any reason, she put her arms round his neck.

'If it's for me to choose, will you please stay here with me?' she said.

He bent his head and gave her a long kiss. Nothing like any kiss he had given her before, and she thought:

'I was right to defy Collier. I was right to fight for my happiness. It's going to mean Charles' happiness too. The loveliest thing that ever happened to either of us.'

*

During the three days of her honeymoon Tina felt there was no one on earth whom she could envy. She even thought, in her moments of most exalted happiness, that if life gave her nothing else but this—if some sort of disastrous exposure awaited her on her return home—still this heavenly little interlude would be worth all the anxiety and fear.

That she could be happy in Charles' company she had always known, but that she should be so wildly, romantically in love with him she had never quite visualised. She had ceased to ask herself if he loved her in the same degree. He loved her in *some* sort of degree, and that was enough.

She realised now that she had never known companionship before and that she had been emotionally lonely for most of her life. With Sonia there had been a certain sense of physical companionship, of course, but they had really had little in common. Whatever there had been between them had lain on the surface of her life. This sharing of thoughts and ideas and experiences with Charles drove deep down to the very roots of her existence.

The odd thing was that they put very little of it into words. They went long walks in the unexpectedly brilliant sunshine which literally illumined their honeymoon for them, and they talked—gaily, casually, teasingly—or were sometimes contentedly silent. But Tina thought that the silence said more than the words—and the actual love passages between them said more than either.

On their last afternoon, when they were strolling through the wooded valley down to the sea, he passed his arm round her, and for a while they walked in silence. Then he said in that tone which meant, she knew, that he was smiling:

'Well, my little wife, was it all rather less terrifying than you expected?'

'Terrifying, Charles? I never expected to be *terrified* on my honeymoon,' she protested.

'No? Well, I've seldom seen you look more anxious and

apprehensive than you did on the journey down,' he told her with amused candour.

'Did I? How ridiculous!' She laughed and flushed. It was impossible, of course, to tell him how many and varied had been her reasons for fear—and that they were certainly not all removed even now. But she pressed his hand against her side and said, 'I couldn't know it would be so heavenly, of course, but I—I don't think I had so many fears as you seem to think.'

'No?' He kissed her cheek in that characteristically careless way which meant, she knew now, something far removed from carelessness. 'Well, promise me at any rate that you'll never be frightened again.'

'Of you?'

'Yes.'

'I'm not frightened of you, Charles. I never was.'

'All right.' He laughed and let her have that point. 'And you're not to be afraid of anyone else either, because I'll deal with anything unpleasant for you in future.'

For a moment she savoured the full delicious sensation of that. Then she smiled—a little wistfully, though she didn't know it—because, of course, the greatest fear of all could never be mentioned to him.

'I'll never let anything frighten me if I think you can deal with it for me,' she promised after a moment. And if he noticed that she had altered the form of words, he said nothing about it.

They left by an early train the next day and arrived in London early enough to snatch a hasty meal with Earle before driving down to the nursing-home.

For some reason or other Earle laughed when he saw them, and said, with his drawl very much pronounced:

'There isn't much need to ask whether married life agrees with you two.'

As they drove down through the early dusk, Tina said contentedly, 'It's lovely to be going home for the very first time, isn't it?'

'Lovely,' Charles agreed with a smile. And then: 'Do

you suppose Mrs Ardingley will expect me to carry you over the front doorstep?'

'That depends entirely on what Sir Thomas did with his lady,' Tina pointed out. 'I feel they probably established a precedent for all time, in Mrs Ardingley's opinion.'

'Hm.' He sounded non-committal. 'Do you want me to?'

'I can bear it if you don't,' Tina assured him, a good deal amused by the almost serious tone of that.

Mrs Ardingley received them rather in the manner of the late Queen Victoria presiding at a Drawing Room, but she was unquestionably pleased to see them.

'Oh, Mrs Ardingley, how nice to have you to come home to!' Tina exclaimed in all sincerity, which caused Mrs Ardingley to bend an extremely benevolent glance upon her.

'Everything all right, Mrs Ardingley?' Charles inquired.

'Everything is perfectly correct and in order, sir,' Mrs Ardingley assured him. 'At least, so far as my own province is concerned. As to the patients—five, I believe, sir, so far—no doubt the Matron or that flighty young person who calls herself Nurse will be better able to report.'

'Nurse Unsworth has every right to the title, you know,' murmured Charles, a good deal amused. 'And, even if she is pretty, she is remarkably efficient.'

Mrs Ardingley pressed her lips together at that, and with an air of producing an entirely new and original remark, observed that handsome was as handsome did, but it was no business of hers.

'Quite right,' agreed Charles with a diplomatically absent air, and it was hard to say whether he was answering the first or the second part of Mrs Ardingley's observation.

But Tina secretly decided, with a slightly guilty feeling, that if she had never liked Mrs Ardingley before, she certainly would have had to now!

As they turned to go upstairs there was a rustle of starched uniform on the upstairs landing, and Eileen appeared at the top of the stairs. She drew back at once, as though surprised to see them, but Tina felt certain that she had timed some errand deliberately, to bring her there as soon as she heard the sound of the car arriving.

Her faintly shy smile of welcome was certainly one of the prettiest things Tina had ever seen. She acknowledged as much to herself with grim amusement. And the sympathetic, 'Oh, you *must* have had a cold journey,' made one feel that Eileen asked nothing better than to minister to one's immediate comfort.

'We survived it,' Charles assured her with a smile. 'How do you like the new quarters?'

'They're simply beautiful. It's hard to believe one's a nurse instead of a guest in the house when everything is done for one's comfort like this!'

'I hope Matron feels as enthusiastic as you,' Charles told her with a dry little smile, as he and Tina turned along the corridor which led to the door cutting off their own wing from the rest of the house.

Tina was not sure why, but as she reached the door, she instinctively glanced back over her shoulder.

Eileen was still standing there at the top of the stairs, looking after them. Or rather, she was looking after Tina. But her expression was no longer shy and pretty. There was a dislike so intense that it amounted to hatred in her eyes, and if anything so pretty could be said to look malevolent, then Eileen did at that moment.

She turned away at once and ran down the stairs, apparently intent on her errand. But as Tina went rather slowly into her new home, she thought:

'That girl isn't to be despised or laughed about, after all. It's not a question of dislike or petty jealousy. I'm up against real hatred!'

CHAPTER TWELVE

TINA was a good deal surprised to find how quickly she slipped into the routine of her new life.

There were days when she saw very little indeed of Charles. Times when he was away at the hospital, operating most of the day. But she was not at all lonely then. After the first feeling of shyness and diffidence, she found herself mixing very happily and easily with the patients in the nursing-home.

Charles had said nothing whatever to her about any share he hoped she would take in the actual work of the home—perhaps because he was not sure how she would react to being surrounded by injured and disfigured people —and undoubtedly his desire to have their own quarters more or less cut off from the rest of the house arose from a determination that she should not be forced into the position of living in circumstances she hated.

But Tina found that, after the first shock of pity and dismay, she was inclined to forget any abnormalities in these people, and she sensed from the beginning that she, perhaps more than anyone else, could help them. She was entirely unconnected with the nursing side of the home. She really belonged to the outside world to which they would eventually return, and she inevitably represented the first link between the rather unnatural circumscribed atmosphere of hospital life and the everyday circumstances which they all slightly dreaded, after their long absence from ordinary routine.

Almost from the first they ceased to be 'patients' to her and became 'guests'. And she found, to her deep and warm satisfaction, that she had a certain instinct which almost always prompted her to handle even the most difficult case correctly.

That all of them owed their recovery to Charles and thought him the most wonderful thing on earth naturally made the first approach specially easy. And it never failed to please her when she was informed that he was 'ever such a wonderful person'.

'Is it against hospital discipline or anything if I encourage them to ask their own families and friends to come and see them here?' she asked Charles after the first week.

'Not if you don't take on more than you can tackle,' he told her with a smile. 'Why? Do most of them say they want that?'

'No,' Tina said slowly. 'That's the most touching thing about them. They're not at all inclined to express their wishes. I think they have some idea that they are under an obligation to us already because they don't pay anything. But there are enough rooms in this house, Charles! Let's have them do a little entertaining on their own—or with me there, if they prefer that. Something quite different from "visiting day" formalities. More like the ordinary intercourse which they will have with people again some day.'

'I leave it in your hands, my dear,' Charles told her, still smiling. 'Don't wear yourself out with enthusiasm, that's all, and allow Matron a certain amount of discipline too. Matrons just slowly fade away if they aren't allowed to exercise any discipline at all.'

Tina laughed and kissed him.

'I'll remember. And thank you, Charles, for letting me have my own way.'

'Don't I always let you have your own way?' he inquired.

'Yes. But I haven't tested you very severely yet, have I?' she countered.

That seemed to amuse him, and he put his arm round her and pulled her down on to the arm of his chair.

'How should you test me, I should like to know?'

She thought of Eileen and she thought of Philip Collier, and found some difficulty in smiling back at him. But she said quite lightly:

'When your husbandly indulgence feels the strain, you can tell me.'

Whereupon he said, 'All right, I will,' rather lazily, and put his head against her.

She looked down at his dark head, and thought, for the first time since she was married, 'Could I dare to tell him, after all? *Could* I?'

Would this easy, good-tempered affection between them stand the strain of quite such a confession? Suppose one were groping for words—what *would* one say?

'I think I ought to tell you that I'm not the person I've pretended to be.' 'I'm not really being generous about that money at all, because not one penny of it is mine. I just swindled you out of it.' 'I couldn't bear to stay in America any longer, so I impersonated someone and pinched a legacy—*your* legacy, incidentally.'

No. None of those sounded very promising openings.

Besides, how could one possibly tell what Charles' reaction would be, even if one put it the very best way possible? Was he one of those rare and blessed people who just love unreasoningly, regardless of a person's character —or was his feeling for people governed by how well or ill he had reason to think of them?

It was impossible to tell. And it would be too late, once one had confessed. That was it—confession was irrevocable. If she gambled on his understanding, and he didn't understand, then she had lost—everything. There wasn't any rubbing out a mistake like that.

'I know what it is,' thought Tina with something like self-contempt, 'my moral nerve has gone. I did something I *knew* was wrong, because I thought I couldn't face the alternative. And now, each time, it seems a little more impossible to do the straight and difficult thing.'

She sighed faintly, and Charles said at once:

'What are you thinking about so hard?' He moved

comfortably against her without even looking up.

'Oh—you, I think.' She smiled involuntarily.

'Good lord! Did I cause that deep sigh?'

'No, no.' She laughed a little then.

'Tell me what you were thinking about me, then.'

'I suppose I was wondering——' She stopped. 'Charles, are you a very forgiving sort of person?'

'That depends what you've been doing,' he said, and glancing down she saw from the curve of his mouth that he was smiling and evidently not taking the query very seriously. 'If you've only broken one of the ornaments, it's all right, but if you've been flirting with someone else— I'm not in the least forgiving.'

'Oh, Charles!' She hoped her laugh didn't sound as troubled to him as it did to her. 'I suppose you mean that small things don't worry you in the least—in this as in every other way—but that you have rather a close regard for the big things.'

'Dear me!' He considered that amusedly. 'Am I really so well-balanced?'

'Of course.' She was quite serious about it. 'I expect that's why you're such a good surgeon.'

'Maybe.' Characteristically he was not the least deprecating about that. 'Anyway, what were you going to confess to me? I'm growing curious.'

'I wasn't going to confess *anything*, Charles!' She was suddenly panic-stricken. 'I was just—just speaking in the most general way. I wasn't thinking of anything particular. You—you mustn't think so.'

'All right.' He laughed good-humouredly. 'You needn't sound so scared.' He glanced up at her mischievously, and she thought how singularly penetrating his eyes were.

She gave him a careless little kiss and stood up, really because she found it hard to meet those shrewd, smiling eyes, even though there was not a trace of real suspicion in them. To him the whole thing was a joke.

And it must remain so! thought Tina. She had been

very silly to make even that general inquiry. Besides, where did it lead? Nothing he could have said, either in joke or in earnest, would really have convinced her that it would be safe to confess.

For a little while after that she found, for some reason or other, that her nervous dread and anxiety became less. Perhaps the reassuring fact that not a word had been heard from Collier had a good deal to do with it, or perhaps it was simply that she was busy and happy in her everyday life and had less time to worry.

For that reason the shock was all the greater when it did come.

It was the afternoon of what was usually one of Charles' 'hospital' days when he was away all day, but on this occasion, owing to some last-minute rearrangement, he had been at home until the early afternoon.

She had enjoyed her morning, going round with him to see their patients, and was specially happy because a very difficult case seemed likely to yield to treatment at last.

'I wish you were staying home this afternoon,' she told him over lunch. 'You're looking just a little tired, Charles, and as though you could do with a rest.'

He shrugged.

'It's nothing. There's been a lot of work lately, but it's not tiring when you're actually doing it. That's the thrilling thing about this comparatively new type of surgery. To-day's discovery may solve the problem of tomorrow's operation. It's endlessly interesting.'

Tina smiled sympathetically and got up to go with him as far as the front door.

As they came out into the corridor which led from their rooms to the head of the stairs, Mrs Ardingley came towards them.

'There is a gentleman to see you, Mrs Linton,' she said, with that faintly prim air of disapproval which usually meant that some hapless visitor had offended against her special code of visitors' behaviour.

'Who is it, Mrs Ardingley?' Tina supposed it was probably someone to see one of the patients who preferred to have a word with her first.

'He wouldn't give his name, madam.' The extra pursing of Mrs Ardingley's lips indicated where the visitor's fault had been.

Tina laughed.

'Never mind, I'll come down.' She glanced past Mrs Ardingley to the trim, pretty figure of Eileen which had just appeared at the top of the stairs. And as she did so, she thought: 'Confound that girl and her spiteful curiosity!' For Eileen was glancing back over her shoulder with particular interest, and evidently would have liked to know more about whoever was standing in the hall.

'Visitors should either hand their card or give their name,' Mrs Ardingley affirmed grimly at that moment, in answer to what she considered to be Tina's too indulgent attitude towards the erring one. 'How is one to know otherwise if one wishes to be "at home"?'

Tina, who was always 'at home' to anyone who wanted to see her, only laughed at that. But Eileen, who had drawn near the group, spoke in a different but helpful way.

'You needn't worry, Mrs Ardingley.' Mrs Ardingley stiffened all over. 'It's a personal friend of Mrs Linton's. The friend you were seeing off at King's Cross that day, Mrs Linton. I recognised him at once.'

Mrs Ardingley's expression said quite plainly that it was the height of impertinence on Eileen's part to have noticed the visitor, much less recognised him, but Tina was not aware of that. She was terrifiedly concerned only with Charles' hasty:

'Well, I must go, my dear. Make my excuses for me, if he was expecting to see your husband. I'm late already.'

She hardly heard the last three words, and instinctively held him back, her hand clutching his arm. She *couldn't* let him go down! He would have to pass Collier in the hall and could not fail to recognise him.

But the astonished look on his face recalled her to a

sense of her peculiar behaviour. Murmuring something—
she hardly knew what—she let him go, and without waiting to say anything more, he just nodded goodbye and ran
down the stairs.

She felt unable even to lean over the banisters and look
after him—see the meeting for herself and judge what
effect it had on Charles. She stood there, a little aimlessly,
vaguely aware that Eileen had turned reluctantly away and
that Mrs Ardingley was obviously waiting for her to go
downstairs.

'I think, madam, he was one of the gentlemen who came
that afternoon to look over the place and ask all those questions,' she explained disapprovingly to Tina. 'I thought I
recognised him, though I couldn't place him. Then when
Nurse Unsworth put *her* oar in, I remembered.'

It was difficult to say why an interruption from Eileen
should have stimulated Mrs Ardingley's memory for something totally unconnected with what she had to say. But
Tina nodded understandingly. She quite realised that an
annoyed competitive spirit had prompted Mrs Ardingley
to supply information in her turn, since Nurse Unsworth
had gone so far out of her own province as to interrupt a
conversation between Mrs Ardingley and her employers.

'I'll come down,' Tina repeated, but in a rather weary
tone. She felt very different from the girl who had said the
same words a few minutes ago.

As she went slowly down the stairs, she realised that
Collier was standing in an embrasure made by one of the
corner windows that jutted out at the side of the house. He
had his back to her, but turned abruptly as he heard her
footsteps across the polished floor of the hall, and for a
moment she had the impression that he too was a good deal
shaken.

Then he hadn't wanted to see Charles either. No, she
supposed, it would be better for his plans that the husband's suspicions should not be aroused just yet.

As she came up to him, she said as naturally as possible:
'How do you do? Did you want to see me?' because she

knew Mrs Ardingley was not far behind her. But the moment she heard the housekeeper's door close behind her, Tina's voice changed to low-toned fury. 'How *dare* you come to this place! Do you think there's nothing that I won't put up with?'

'You haven't much choice, have you?' he retorted rudely. But he was not so sure of himself today, and when she made as though to speak again, he interrupted her a trifle sullenly. 'All right, all right. You don't suppose I would have come if it hadn't been urgent, do you? I didn't specially want to run into that husband of yours. Damned bad luck that he should come down just then. I thought this was his day for operating over at the hospital. I rang up specially to make sure.'

It was useless to comment on the effrontery of that, so she just said briefly:

'There was a rearrangement. He's only just gone now. Did he—did he recognise you?—speak to you?'

'I don't know if he recognised me.' Collier was uneasy although he tried to cover the fact. 'I turned and looked out of the window, the moment I realised who it was, and he passed without attempting to speak. But I couldn't say if he knew me. You'll have to lie pretty smartly if he asks questions.'

'What am I doing?' thought Tina, furious and miserable. 'Arranging with this devil of a man how we shall cheat Charles between us!' But there was no time for protest now, and aloud she simply said:

'What have you come for?'

'Can't we go somewhere a little less public and talk?' he asked irritably, and she was more sure than ever that he was shaken by having so nearly encountered Charles face to face. If only one could threaten in one's own turn! It was so hard that Charles—of whom this man was really afraid —should be the very one to whom she could not appeal.

She would have liked to refuse to fall in with his suggestion, but for her own sake she must comply. If Eileen were to contrive to come down again on one of her innumerable and useful errands, there was no saying what she might deduce.

Without a word, Tina led the way into a small sitting-room where she usually received the friends and relations who came to see her patients. How she wished it were someone as welcome and harmless whom she was interviewing now!

The measure of privacy seemed to restore Collier's self-confidence immediately. He took a chair without being asked to do so, and looked round him with a disagreeable smile.

'Pretty comfortable here, aren't you?' he said approvingly.

'Was that what you came to tell me?' Tina asked crisply, and he laughed.

'No,' he drawled. 'I came to let you know how very useful that little present was that you gave me. Saw me through a difficult week or two, I can tell you. But——'

'I'm not interested in what you did with the money you blackmailed out of me,' she interrupted fiercely.

'No. But this bit *will* interest you. I was unlucky and—lost the last fifty pounds.'

'Lost it?' She looked at him with contempt.

'Um-hm. There are various ways of losing money, you know. Sometimes one makes an unlucky bet.'

'Oh—that!' Her scorn deepened. Then she pressed her lips together. 'What has that to do with me?'

'Quite a lot, my dear, because, by a series of circumstances with which I won't bore you, I need fifty pounds very, very urgently. You're my best chance of getting it. That's why I'm down here this afternoon, in spite of the risk of running into your charming husband.'

'Do you suppose,' Tina asked slowly and coldly, 'that every time you want a sum of money, large or small, you have only to come here whining to me?'

'Demanding,' he corrected almost pleasantly.

'Whichever way you put it, you must see that the position is impossible!' she exclaimed. 'No one would—*could* put up with it. Whether I—I thought it worth while or not, I should have to tell my husband. I simply couldn't stand it.'

She saw that her words really made some impression on him. He sat up slowly from his lounging position, studying her with that frankly insolent gaze.

'Well, I see your point,' he said with an air of mocking reasonableness. 'But that isn't my idea, you know. You won't be having so many visits from me.' Her heart leapt with hope. 'This is what you might term a little emergency call. But when I have time to get down to our problem properly—well, we've never had that long talk, you and I, and when we do, I think we should be able to come to something quite satisfactory between us—something which means I don't have to bother you like this.'

'You—you mean a sort of settlement?' She hated herself for catching so eagerly at his monstrous hint.

He grinned at her and nodded.

Tina said nothing for a moment. She was breathless with the glimpse of freedom at last. Whatever it cost her, she felt she would pay it thankfully. If this wretch meant that he would take a large sum and clear out—leave England—then it would be worth anything.

'When do you propose to have this—this "little talk", as you call it?' She tried—unsuccessfully, she felt—to conceal her eagerness.

'Oh, I don't know.' He considered the point carelessly, and she felt furiously sure that he was certain he could make his own terms. 'Shall we say—Friday week?'

'That's nearly a fortnight to wait.' Her voice was sharper than she meant it to be.

'But I can't manage it before then,' he retorted at once, with an air of finality that just prevented her from descending to argument.

'Friday week, then,' she said shortly. 'And for the present——?'

'For the present?—fifty pounds,' he told her smilingly.

She said nothing. There was really nothing to say. All

she could do was go out of the room, with what dignity she could muster, and upstairs to her own room to fetch the money this man demanded.

Tina was almost surprised that she saw nothing of Eileen either on the way up or when she was coming back. It would have been entirely in character if Eileen had managed—most charmingly and convincingly, of course— to be somewhere handy to observe Tina's preoccupation and distress.

As it was, she returned safely to the room where Collier was waiting—on his feet now, and with an air of not wanting to wait any longer. Perhaps the few minutes alone had given him time to think over how awkward it would be if some accident should bring Charles back again.

He took the money without any touch of shame, counted it, and put it away in his wallet.

'Thanks,' he said, as though she had been paying a debt. 'And I'll let you know when and where to meet me on Friday week.'

Tina didn't waste any goodbyes on him. She saw him to the door, closing it behind him almost before he had left the front step. Then, feeling very tired, she went slowly upstairs.

But she changed her mind about going to her own room. It was impossible to bear one's own thoughts this afternoon. And she went to see some of the patients instead.

Their company and their conversation quieted her nerves a little, though from time to time she remembered with sickening apprehension that Charles would be coming home some time, and if he had indeed seen Collier he would be bound to expect some explanation.

And that odious, odious remark of Eileen's! How could Charles be anything but suspicious if he had really recognised Collier and now knew, thanks to Eileen, that he was the man Tina had been with at King's Cross!

More than once that afternoon, she knew, Eileen's large thoughtful eyes regarded her with innocent interest and curiosity. Audrey herself could not have looked more art-

less, but Tina knew that behind that innocent stare, inquisitive and uncharitable ideas were working.

It made her feel slightly hysterical—as though she must
justify herself aggressively to Eileen, without even being
accused. That would be insane, of course, but the desire
to try to find out something of Eileen's thoughts became
irresistible.

As she was leaving to go across to her own rooms, she
noticed that Eileen was going off duty, and on the split of
the moment she said:

'Do come across and have tea with me, will you? It's
rather quiet on my own.'

There was only a moment's hesitation before Eileen
accepted with a graceful:

'Thank you, I'd love to.'

For the first few minutes it was difficult to know how
to make conversation. Then tea was brought in, and over
the usual conventional inquiries and answers the restraint
between them lessened.

Tina wondered a little now why she had forced that
meeting, and then it gradually became apparent to her that
Eileen was much more ill at ease than she herself. It was
difficult to imagine why, for Eileen was not a girl who was
easily put out.

If she had not wanted to come, she could easily have
made some excuse. But it was more than a general reluct-
ance to be in the society of someone she envied and disliked, Tina thought. There was a sort of wariness about
her, which no charm and smiling self-assurance could
efface. As though she, and not Tina, had reason to be
anxious.

For a while Tina was completely mystified. Then Eileen
said, with all the casualness in the world:

'It was very nice of you to let Audrey come to your
wedding. She was terribly thrilled, you know. But then—
you really got very friendly with my young sister, didn't
you?'

'Yes.'

'Mrs Linton, she's also a very tiresome child at times.' Eileen's expression was that of an indulgent elder sister rather than the domestic tyrant which Tina knew she could be to poor young Audrey. 'She's very much inclined to exaggerate and even—romance about people. I think you must have noticed it sometimes.'

The indulgent expression vanished suddenly, and she was looking very hard at Tina—almost challengingly.

'Ah,' thought Tina, 'now I know what's wrong! She's got it out of poor Audrey that there's been some injudicious talk!'

'Audrey never told me anything that struck me as—untruthful,' she said pleasantly, though a little dangerously. 'And I'm not sure that she even exaggerated, more than girls of her age often do.'

'Mrs Linton, she said some extremely exaggerated—and untrue—things about me, I think.'

'What makes you think that?' inquired Tina with a coolness that did her credit.

'I don't even *think* it—I *know* it,' Eileen retorted impatiently. And with that sudden gesture of frankness the formal relationship of nurse and surgeon's wife ceased to exist between them. They were just two girls who very much disliked each other because of one man. 'Audrey confessed some of the—the ridiculous things she told you about me. She made some silly remark which made me suspicious, and then I made her tell me what she had been saying.'

'But were they such very ridiculous things that she told me?' Tina said quietly, wondering *en passant* how much sisterly bullying had gone to making Audrey disclose what she had said.

'Of course they were!' Eileen sounded as though she were controlling her temper with difficulty. 'Stupid things about me and——'

'About you and my husband,' Tina completed for her.

'Exactly. That I intended——'

'Eileen,' Tina said unexpectedly, 'don't you think it

would be much better for your dignity and our future relationship if you didn't put these things into words? Just as it would have been much better for you not to have accepted the post at this particular nursing-home. You're attractive—my husband says you are an excellent nurse. You could go anywhere.'

'I see you refuse to believe anything but what that little idiot told you!' Eileen exclaimed indignantly. 'I suppose you *like* to think that other women are running after your husband! It makes you feel good to think that *you* got him.'

'It may surprise you to know that I never regarded Charles in that interesting light,' Tina said dryly.

Eileen whitened slowly—with sheer temper, Tina felt sure—and her usual self-control seemed to crack all over, like thin enamel.

'You smug, self-satisfied woman!'

'Be quiet!'

Tina held up her hand for silence—not because she so much resented what was said, but because the door behind Eileen had opened and Charles stood in the doorway, surveying the scene with some astonishment.

But Eileen meant to say what was in her mind now, irrespective of whether the detested wife liked it or not. And, ignoring Tina's gesture, she rushed on in a furious flood of low-toned but clear speech.

'How long do you suppose *you* will hold him? You can't even appreciate his work. You and your boy-friends who meet you at railway stations and come snooping round here without giving a name!'

There was a perfectly terrible little silence for a few seconds after that. Then it was Charles, and not Tina, who broke it.

'I think, Nurse, that Matron wants you,' he said very coolly indeed.

Eileen switched round, white to the lips, and at the sight of Charles she pressed the back of her hand against her mouth, as though even now she would try to keep back the words which had been all too clearly said.

Then, as though she suddenly realised that she had completely done for herself and might as well injure Tina as much as possible, she started to speak again.

'I'm sorry you heard what I said. But there's a great deal more that you ought to hear. Do you know that——'

'Nurse Unsworth'—Charles regarded his admirably shaped finger-nails with attention—'I think I have already heard more than I ought to hear, and I'm sure you won't want to keep Matron waiting.'

She gave a little gasp that was almost a sob of rage. Then, with a look like daggers at Tina, she fled from the room.

Charles came slowly forward and held out his hands to the fire, while Tina watched him in fascinated silence.

'Pity,' he said at last. 'She was a good nurse.'

'What—do you mean?'

'That I'll have to find another one equally good.'

Illogically Tina felt faintly sorry for Eileen. Her world must have crashed so completely.

'She was rather overwrought,' she murmured at last.

'Obviously.'

'Charles, girls do sometimes get silly like that about——'

'I'll recommend her to our senior ear, nose, and throat man. He's the safe side of sixty. And there's nothing like perpetual tonsillectomy for reducing romantic excesses.'

Tina laughed slightly.

'I feel a little guilty. I said something which provoked her. You see——'

'I don't think it matters what you said, my dear. I shouldn't dream of keeping in the house anyone who spoke to you like that. Besides'—he frowned—'stupid of me not to have noticed before. It doesn't matter.' And then, quite casually, 'Did your caller stay long?'

'N-no.' In the agitation of this scene with Eileen, Tina had almost forgotten the much greater worry.

She glanced sharply at her husband now, trying to read from his expression whether he had recognised Collier and was indulging in some disagreeable wondering now. Nothing in his face suggested that. In fact, it was singularly blank of expression. And suddenly that frightened Tina much more than anything else could have done. In the ordinary way, Charles' face was so lively and expressive that there was something strange and disquieting about that slightly blank look. As though he were deliberately controlling any expression in case it should be the wrong one.

She tried to tell herself that she was imagining things— that her stupid fears were preventing her from enjoying any relief even when there *was* some. But a deep, inner instinct told her that Charles had seen her visitor and knew there was something wrong.

Then why not question her?

She waited, breathless, for some question, unaware that her uncommunicative reply was a little surprising in itself. She was past making herself try to say the natural thing— invent some conversation about an imaginary visitor in the hope that all was still well, in spite of her inner misgiving.

But no question came. Charles seemed inclined to let the subject drop. But then he seemed equally disinclined to take up any other. And that was unlike him. He was usually rather amusing when the day's work was over and he could relax in his own home again.

Suddenly she felt that *she* must touch on the subject, even if he would not.

But how?

If she staked everything on his not knowing who her visitor was, and told some easy, convincing little fibs, he would know immediately that something was seriously wrong—if he *had* recognised Collier.

The silence lengthened—unnaturally, it seemed to her. And then she rather desperately tackled the subject from another angle.

'Charles—I don't know how much you heard of what Eileen was saying——'

'More than enough,' he assured her dryly.

'Then I feel—since you heard her accuse me—I ought to explain that——'

'For God's sake don't explain anything!' Charles exclaimed more violently than he had ever spoken to her. 'If you don't want to tell me anything about some concern of yours, I certainly don't want to hear of it by way of Eileen Unsworth's catty insinuations. Let's leave the subject alone. Anything I ought to hear about you, I suppose I shall hear from you yourself. I certainly don't need the assistance of my nursing staff in understanding my wife.'

And abruptly he went into his own room, leaving her to wonder, with chilly anxiety, whether his violence were prompted by a certain anger with her, or an indignant desire to disclaim any idea of suspecting her.

Tina sat down slowly by the fire and put her head in her hands.

In whatever way he had meant them, those words, 'Anything I ought to hear about you, I suppose I shall hear from you yourself,' cut very deep indeed.

He *trusted* her to tell him. And she couldn't.

To Tina that really was the bitterest moment yet. And the thought that there was no end——

'But there *will* be an end!'—she reminded herself with desperate hope. 'Collier means to take all he can and get out. That's what he meant. That's what he *must* have meant! Oh, I hardly care what it costs, if only he goes.'

She wondered if she were building too much on what was little more than a strong hint. But the word 'settlement' had been used. He *couldn't* mean anything else. She couldn't bear it if he meant something else.

And to Tina it seemed that, disagreeable though that 'little talk' with Collier must be, it represented the brightest hope she had ever known.

CHAPTER THIRTEEN

To Tina the next ten days were a nightmare, only brightened by the singularly undramatic departure of Eileen.

She never knew how Charles managed it so tactfully, but Eileen left, with nothing more than a slight ripple of regret from one or two of the patients who thought her 'sweet'. Certainly there was no breath of scandal about the whole arrangement—only the vague suggestion that certain private affairs of Nurse Unsworth made it inconvenient for her to be nursing outside London, after all.

'And though it's not for me to say, madam,' remarked Mrs Ardingley—determined to say it all the same, 'she is *not* what one might call a loss to anyone.'

'I think she was very popular with the patients, Mrs Ardingley,' Tina said diplomatically.

'I've been in the world a lot longer than you and I've *seen* things. And *I* know trouble when I meet it, be it never so smiling and dressed up. Nurse Unsworth isn't a new type. They had her kind in the Garden of Eden. And we all know how much bother *that* caused.'

And, smiling grimly to herself at her rare little joke, Mrs Ardingley took herself off with an extremely satisfied expression.

'I wonder,' thought Tina amusedly, 'whether she was casting poor Eileen for Eve or the Serpent. A mixture of the two, I dare say. Well, at least she was right about one thing. Eileen was trouble incarnate.'

And now she was gone. If only one could savour the full, delightful relief of that!

'But everything will be all right, once I've seen Collier

for the last time and—paid him off,' Tina assured herself feverishly. 'I can be happy and feel free. Oh, the day he goes back to Canada will be the happiest of my life! For of course he will go back. He *must* go back. He was only here on a visit, when all's said and done. Only he's succeeded in frightening me so dreadfully that he means to make every penny he can before he has to go back. Perhaps,' she thought forlornly, 'it's largely bluff really. And if I defy him——'

But she knew she was not prepared to defy him on any real scale. She would pay and be thankful. And then at last she would be free.

Of course if his demands were exorbitant, there would be the difficulty of explaining to Charles sometime why her capital was so seriously depleted. But she couldn't think of that now. Some explanation would offer itself. And even if Charles had to think her a bit of a fool where money matters were concerned, that was better—ten thousand times better—than that he should know the truth.

Her conscience prompted her then to remember that it was really Charles' money with which she proposed to deal so lavishly. But then it was Charles' happiness, too, which she was trying to save. She hoped wearily that the one cancelled out the other.

During this time she watched with the most acute anxiety for any change in Charles' manner towards her—any sign that although he refused to voice his suspicions, they were there all the time. But there was nothing which could cause her real fear. He was rather more than usually preoccupied sometimes, but then she knew he was also overwhelmingly busy. And if he had a little less time for her than usual, he also had less time for anything else that did not directly concern his work.

She assured herself that any possible suspicion there had been had died long ago, and once she could dispose of Philip Collier and his demands, there was nothing that need stand in the way of their growing happiness.

To her immeasurable relief, Charles was out of the house

when Collier finally telephoned to make arrangements for meeting her.

But her relief turned to dismay when he said:

'I must see you at once.'

'Do you mean this evening?' for it was already late in the afternoon.

'I mean this evening.'

'But I *can't*! It would mean having to stay in town for the night. What possible explanation could I give? It would sound——'

'I don't care what explanation you give. Think up something convincing. Good lord, use your imagination, girl! It's necessary that I see you and come to—some arrangement at once.'

With a sudden wild hope she told herself that could mean only one thing. He had to go back immediately! That was the reason for the haste.

Then it was worth it! She would make up some story that would cover it. She could stay at her old hotel for the night. It was fairly simple, after all.

'I'll come. Where shall I meet you?'

She knew from his exclamation that he had expected more protests and was pleasantly surprised by her capitulation.

'Sensible girl,' he approved. 'Do you know a little street called Maltry Street off the King's Road?'

'I can find it.'

'There's a restaurant there that stays open late. You'll know it by the red door and a couple of shrubs outside in tubs. I'll meet you there at nine.'

'Nine!'

'Yes. I can't manage before then.'

It was pointless to argue over details now.

'Very well, I'll be there.'

She rang off, strangely excited and almost exhilarated now that the final moment was so near. It wouldn't be long now—it wouldn't be long—before she was free.

She hastily packed the few things she would need for a

night in town, and then called Mrs Ardingley.

'Mrs Ardingley, tell Mr Linton I was called away suddenly, but I'll be back some time before lunch tomorrow. A very old friend from the States has just telephoned to say she's passing through London and she managed to get hold of my address.' (Tina hoped neither of them would wonder how!) 'She wants me to go up and have dinner with her this evening. I shouldn't like to miss her.'

'You'll have to stay in town for the night?' Mrs Ardingley was very disapproving.

'Yes. Tell Mr Linton that I'll stay at my old hotel for the night, and if he's still up at—oh, twelve—he can ring me there if he likes.'

She thought how wonderful it would be just to hear Charles' voice, when all this misery was over.

'Very well, madam.' Mrs Ardingley spoke in the manner of one who must withhold approval but who realised that she was powerless to alter things.

Tina smiled at her in a way that really did suggest she expected to have a good time. And then she went off to her final meeting with Collier.

Audrey, she found to her relief, was out of London for a day or two. So there was no need to explain her presence— or, still worse, be questioned about her version of the Eileen incident.

Somewhat to her surprise she enjoyed her dinner, and it was with a genuine effort that she kept her spirits from mounting dangerously high.

She took a taxi to Chelsea and as it hurtled round corners and negotiated bends Tina slid about on the cold, shiny upholstery and wondered if she would arrive at her destination with enough breath to deal with Philip Collier. But presently the cab drew up in the little street off the King's Road.

A dull red sign indicated that the restaurant was indeed open, and once inside, Tina found that it was not an uncheerful place. The chairs and tables were of unpolished white wood, but the gay red-and-white check cloths and the small vases of flowers made pleasant splashes of colour.

One or two couples were scattered about the room, leaning towards each other across the tables and speaking in the low, urgent tones of people who want to talk privately but have nowhere really private to go. Sweethearts, most of them, Tina judged, as she sat down at a corner table and ordered coffee while she waited.

A few minutes later the door opened and Philip Collier came into the restaurant.

He stood there for a moment, blinking slightly in the bright light after the darkness. Then he saw her and came straight across, smiling in a way that was all the more disquieting because it would have appeared so cordial to the casual observer.

'You're very punctual.' He dropped into the seat opposite her.

'Yes. I saw no reason for not getting this over as quickly as possible,' she retorted crisply.

'You do dislike me, don't you?' he said.

'I have no reason to like you,' Tina pointed out coldly.

'No? But I've kept your secret very snug and quiet, so far. You might show a little gratitude for that, I think.'

'For a matter of common or garden blackmail, you take a long while to come to the point.'

'Blackmail is a very ugly word, my dear.'

'It's also a very ugly thing,' Tina said dryly. 'And the sentence for it is perhaps the ugliest of all.'

He laughed scornfully in his turn.

'But then I shan't have to worry about that,' he pointed out with a confidence which she envied him, 'because the sentence for murder is uglier still.'

She paled, but more with anger than with fear this time.

'You're wasting time by trying to raise that ridiculous bogy,' she told him. 'You know there isn't—isn't a shred of evidence against me.'

'Or for you,' he said meditatively, staring down into his coffee-cup. 'Only the fact that your friend disappeared in absolutely unprovable circumstances, and that you turned up later, impersonating her and gathering in her quite considerable inheritance.'

'The most fantastic efforts won't make a murder story out of that,' Tina retorted shortly, aware that, low though their voices were, the very bandying of these preposterous words made her wince.

'No?' He looked considering. 'But it makes a very nasty story for the ears of a new husband.'

Tina bit her lip until she felt the blood come. There was the rub, of course! A very nasty story for the ears of a husband.

Collier never took his eyes off her. He knew in a moment when he had scored a point.

'How—how much would you expect to get for clearing out of this country and never setting foot here again?'

'For what?' He laughed contemptuously. 'But, my dear girl, I *like* your charming country. Why should I leave it?'

Her lips were suddenly terribly dry.

'I thought you were here on a visit? That you meant to —leave?'

'I was,' he agreed carelessly. 'And I did. But a visit can always be extended, particularly if one is a journalist and, even more particularly, if one is on to a good thing.'

Tina felt a wave of the most utter despair engulf her. This was not to be the end then. However heavily she paid now, she was not going to purchase security at all. Only the cessation of these week-to-week demands—because it suited him better this way. She had been deluding herself quite uselessly. He didn't mean her to escape with a final payment, however large. He reserved the right to call on her again in the future—even though it might be a fairly distant future.

With an effort Tina concentrated her thoughts on what he was saying. If she had the thinnest, faintest hope of outwitting him, she must at least have all her attention on him.

'Hadn't you better put your proposals yourself?' she suggested. 'Then I'll tell you what I think of them.'

'Always bearing in mind how awkward certain disclosures would be for you,' he reminded her sneeringly.

'Possibly. But there's such a thing as choosing the lesser of two evils, you know. If you make your—your terms too unbearable I shall probably choose to—to tell my husband myself.'

'A lot for a husband to swallow,' Collier pointed out smoothly. 'And I have some idea he might cease to occupy that happy position if he knew the truth.'

Tina paled, but she said nothing, and Collier went on meditatively:

'Few men would like to think their wife might have to face a charge of swindling.'

'No charge would be brought,' Tina retorted curtly. Of that, at least, she was sure.

'Oh?' His eyebrows went up amusedly. 'What makes you so sure of that?'

'Charles would never—would never bring a charge against me.'

'*He* wouldn't? What has he got to do with it?'

Tina looked at her tormentor in surprise. Then she saw he was really unaware of one of the most important facts.

'Don't you realise that my husband would have inherited the money if—if Sonia Frayne had not?'

'Is—that—so?' he said slowly, and she saw that, momentarily, he was slightly put off, that he believed his case to be weakened. She pressed her advantage at once.

'So you see'—she smiled at him coolly and scornfully— 'you do *not* hold the threat of—of police proceedings over me.'

He narrowed his eyes thoughtfully.

'No. But the injury against your precious Charles Linton is infinitely greater than I thought,' he retorted triumphantly.

Tina bit her lip. She guessed that his more offensive way of referring to Charles probably meant that he was slightly less sure of himself. But even allowing for that, the devil still had it in his power to wreck her life.

'And once he had withdrawn his interest,' Collier went

on, as though following her own train of thought, 'there wouldn't be anyone to help you if I had some nasty inquiries instituted. No, no, Miss—Frayne. I should say—Mrs Linton! I think my silence must still have a pretty high value to you.'

She saw that what she had almost imagined to be a way of escape was nothing but a blind alley after all.

'How much?' she asked abruptly.

'Five thousand,' he said, just as abruptly as she had.

'Five thousand?' She was almost relieved to find it was not twice that amount. 'But——'

'That should do for quite a long time,' he explained smoothly, and every hope that had raised its head promptly died.

'What do you mean—"for quite a long time"?'

'That it's always a mistake to accept a lump sum when one can make it an income for life,' was the cool reply.

She sat there thinking that over in a numb and wretched way. The complete confirmation of all her worst fears.

There was no escape—but there *must* be.

'I couldn't agree to that,' she said flatly at last.

'To the five thousand, you mean?'

'To any arrangement which left you free to—to bleed me when you liked. So that I never had any sense of security or freedom.'

He shrugged and smiled at her, but she thought she had never seen anything so hard as his eyes.

'You bother too much about the future, my dear. Perhaps I'll be lucky with the five thousand, and never have to ask you to—oblige me again.'

'Lucky? Lucky? What do you mean? Do you gamble with *any* money you get hold of?' She looked at him with more lively distaste than ever, for she saw the endless, dreary path that stretched in front of them.

He shrugged again. And after a moment she said:

'If I—if I gave you this five thousand, I couldn't guarantee there would ever be any more, you know. This nursing-home that we've started—it takes a lot of money and probably will take still more. We didn't reckon to run it on a profit-paying basis. We meant——'

She stopped suddenly and caught a trembling lip between her teeth. Because they had meant it to be so beautiful and idealistic. They had meant to run that home for the sake of poor, suffering humanity. And now its very foundations were threatened by the filthy grip of a blackmailer. For a wild moment she wondered if she could explain to him—make him see. But she knew, of course, that it was impossible. A man who could do what he was doing would have no interest in hopes and ideals. Even as she wondered he said dryly:

'I think you will usually be able to find any money I need.'

'But if I have none *left*?' She could visualise that sickening day so clearly. Perhaps some years hence—but inevitably there in the future—the day when she could no longer satisfy this terrible man, and when she would have probably even more to lose than now, if exposure came.

'You forget that your husband is a coming man,' Collier told her coolly. 'A man who will make a great deal of money as time goes on. A successful surgeon always does, you know. You will have a big allowance of your own—if you play your cards well. Certainly enough to cover any little indiscretion that may——'

'*No!*'

Tina got to her feet. 'No! I won't have Charles drawn into this.'

Collier grabbed her by the arm. 'There's no need to get excited.'

'Excited!' Tina laughed wretchedly. Suddenly she felt she must spring to her feet and get away from this dreadful man. Hardly knowing what she was doing, she brushed Collier aside and ran for the door, wrenching it open and running into the blessedly cool air of the street outside. Aware of a startled cry behind her and the sound of Collier in hot pursuit, Tina ran out into the King's Road, driven by a blind desire to escape.

The sudden screech of brakes and the sound of a horn blaring brought an awareness of danger too late to help her. There was the sudden pain of something striking her side and then darkness.

CHAPTER FOURTEEN

WHEN Tina came to herself again she was lying in a white-painted bed in a small, pleasant room with windows high up in the walls. She thought from the light that it must be evening, and from the sound of subdued bustle outside the room that she must be in a hospital.

This might be the big accident hospital where Charles did so much of his work, and if so, he couldn't be far away and she would see him soon.

She lay there quietly for a long time, thinking things over. The terrible agitation and confusion of that scene in the restaurant had passed. She could think quite coolly now, and she wondered, not for the first time, what had happened to Philip Collier.

Tina sighed and moved her heavily bandaged arm. She was not quite sure whether it was her arm that ached, or something right deep down inside her.

Then the door opened and Charles came in, and she forgot about her arm or anything else.

He looked tired, she thought, as he bent over her to kiss her. Tired, and something more than his age. It was the first time she had ever seen his magnificent vitality dimmed, and she said irresistibly:

'Charles dear, you look worn out.'

He smiled slightly.

'Do I? Well, I've had a rather wearing twenty-four hours.'

'Poor man! You must have. I'm sorry to have given you all that anxiety. But I'm getting better now. I'll soon be all right.'

'Yes, you'll soon be all right.' He touched her fair hair lightly but very tenderly.

She wondered if he would ask her what she had been doing in that little Chelsea restaurant, and above all, why Philip Collier had been there. But he said nothing, and after a moment she asked:

'How did you know where I was?'

'I phoned the hotel when I got back home last night and Mrs Ardingley gave me your message. I was frantic with worry when they said you'd gone out and hadn't got back yet, although it was after midnight. I caught the first train to Town and started ringing round the hospitals. You were brought in last night.'

She frowned, trying to remember. 'I ran in front of a car. I was trying to get away from Collier. He—he ran after me. I thought he was going to catch me.'

Charles' face was grim. 'The car that swerved in an attempt to avoid you hit him. He was brought in here, but died shortly after. He couldn't have suffered at all.'

'Like a judgment,' Tina whispered, and felt, rather than saw, that Charles glanced at her curiously.

'Like a judgment, eh?' he said slowly at last. 'So that was it.'

She thought, then, he must surely ask for more details, but he seemed either totally incurious or determined not to ask questions she might not want to answer. The escape was complete—if she chose to take it. She knew instinctively that he would never mention Collier again if she didn't. Not Collier's death, but Charles' generosity, was her complete salvation. He would accept the truth or a lie—just as she cared to give it to him.

It was for her to choose.

'Charles——' Nervously she fingered one of his cuff-links.'

'Yes?'

'You don't ask me what I was doing in that place with— with Collier.'

There was an odd little pause. Then he said:

'I'm sure you had your very good reasons for being there. You don't have to tell me if you don't want to.'

'I don't—have—to tell—you?'

'Not,' he repeated slowly, 'if you don't want to.'

It was not even necessary to lie—in so many words. Only to go on living that lie, secure in the knowledge that Charles would neither listen to nor believe anything that was said against her. It was the most complete get-out that had ever been offered to anyone. No shred of reason existed now for her to confess to him.

And in that moment she knew suddenly that she *must* tell him. Just because there was no compulsion any more— only the fact that if her love for him were worth anything she must be as generous and as frank as he. Otherwise their life together would mean nothing.

If he weighed the facts and judged against her—well, then she had lost. But it was for him to say. She had fought and schemed and agonised over her choice, believing until this very moment that the choice was hers. But she was wrong. The choice was not hers at all. It was his.

'Don't tremble so,' his voice said quietly, and only then did she know how agitated she was.

She looked up at him piteously, and at the expression on his face she suddenly flung her arm round his neck and began to weep.

'I love you so, Charles! I love you *terribly*! I can't go on.'

'Hush, darling, hush.' He was kissing her and holding her very close. 'Of course you love me. I know you do— I've known it for a long time now. But you must know I love you too. Why do you say you can't go on? Why shouldn't this marriage of ours go on—to the last degree of living happy ever after?'

'Oh, it's not the marriage,' she said with a little gasp. 'You don't understand.'

'No, I know I don't. I'm probably being dreadfully stupid.' He kissed the top of her head again, as though she were a child. 'But perhaps you're going to make me understand, eh?'

'Yes.' That came in a whisper.

He waited patiently, although her explanation was still some time coming. Then, when it came, it opened with the one devastating truth:

'I'm not Sonia Frayne at all.'

There was a short silence. Then he said:

'Aren't you? But what the devil does it matter? Do you think I love you for your name? I never liked "Sonia" in any case. What *is* your name?'

She felt she was being sidetracked from the dreadful confession, but she could only answer a question put with so much affectionate curiosity.

'Tina,' she said in a small whisper.

For some reason he laughed a good deal at that.

'How sweet and silly! But it suits you ten thousand times better than Sonia.'

'Because I'm sweet and silly?' she felt bound to ask, though her smile was very wan.

'No.' He kissed her. 'It's a dear little name. I like it. Is that all the terrible confession amounts to?'

'Oh, Charles—don't you see? I—I *impersonated* Sonia Frayne. I—I took the money.'

'Oh, the deuce! So you did.' He made a grimace. 'How entirely ridiculous of you—apart from any moral question. Did you really imagine you had the makings of a successful criminal?'

'Charles, it's not in the least funny.' She buried her face against him, half in distress and half relief that he could still be sufficiently amused to tease her.

'No, I see it's really a confoundedly serious business. How much do we owe the genuine Sonia Frayne?'

'*We?*' She looked up in astonishment. 'What have you got to do with this?'

'Well, what do you think I have to do with it?' He smiled down at her. 'Isn't it my business to get you out of the shocking fix you've plunged into?'

She stared at him incredulously. Then she said slowly:

'Would you really stand by me to that extent?'

'Of course.' He was serious now.

'Even to the point of—of helping me to escape the consequences of—a crime?'

He wrinkled his forehead thoughtfully.

'I suppose I'm not taking the crime part very seriously. I just *know* you aren't the criminal type, child. You've just got yourself mixed up in some unholy mess—and I suppose Collier had something to do with it,' he added grimly.

'Charles, do you realise what you are saying?'

'Eh?' He looked rather puzzled.

She pressed against him suddenly, as though his warmth and vitality were something that gave her strength too.

'What you said meant that—that you hardly cared how wicked I'd been. You just didn't believe it because you loved me.'

He narrowed those bright, usually smiling eyes of his slightly.

'All right, I suppose that about describes it. Have you perhaps forgotten that I nearly lost you last night? A few hours like that do a lot to clarify one's thoughts, you know. One finds out the very few things that really matter. You're one of them, that's all.'

He was perfectly serious. He was not even dramatic about it. The facts, for him, were just as he gave them.

Tina put up her hand against his cheek, with an odd little caress which was more tender than anything else she had ever done.

'Charles, no wonder I love you.'

He laughed and flushed slightly.

'Well, how do you think I could help loving you, come to that?'

'By knowing the truth about me, I thought,' she confessed with a sigh.

'You thought I should stop loving you because of this ridiculous Sonia Frayne business?'

'Most men would.'

'I'm not concerned with "most men". Their reactions don't interest me,' he said with perfect truth, and she realised with a little smile of relief that that was so. Charles was completely independent of what one should do or think —or what other people would do or think. He had his own standards and his own scale of values, and he followed them—arrogantly sometimes but with absolute sincerity.

After that, somehow, there was very little difficulty in explaining about her friendship with Sonia, her desperate longing to come home, and the sudden incredible chance which was offered.

He listened quietly and without any interruption while she told him about Sonia's offer, followed immediately by Sonia's tragic death. His only comment was:

'So there is no Sonia Frayne really?'

'No.' Tina shook her head. 'That's why it's really *you* that I've been defrauding all the time, you see.'

'*Me?*' Charles regarded her in astonishment. Then he threw his head back and laughed and laughed.

'Oh, Charles, it's nothing to laugh at,' she protested. 'It's such an awful thing to have done.'

'I should say it is—now that I recognise myself as the victim,' he agreed amusedly.

'But the—the money is yours now,' she pleaded anxiously.

'What's left of it,' he pointed out teasingly.

'I—haven't spent much,' she whispered. 'Except on the nursing-home. And I thought—I thought——'

'Oh, darling!' The teasing expression was gone suddenly, to be succeeded by one of the utmost tenderness. 'Was *that* why you were so anxious for me to have my nursing-home?'

'Not only that.' Tina spoke in a low voice. 'At least, that was the main idea at first. But when I understood—I wanted it so much too, Charles. It was such a wonderful idea. Even if the money had been mine, dear, you should have had it for just that purpose. It—it isn't mine. It's your money and your nursing-home. But I wanted you to have it. Oh, Charles, I wanted you so much to have it.'

'I see.' He was perfectly grave now. 'I do understand.

But it isn't mine, you know, or yours. It's ours—in trust.'

'In trust?'

'Yes,' he said slowly, and he used the expression which had passed through her own mind only last night. 'In trust for poor, suffering humanity.'

'Charles! Is that how *you* feel? I thought somehow that you—that you——'

'Yes? What did you think about me?'

'That money was rather important to you. I even heard it said once that you declared you would marry for money.'

'Well, didn't I do just that?' But his smile was graver than usual.

'Not in that sense.'

'No.' He put his cheek thoughtfully against her hair. 'I suppose there was a time when I might well have done just that,' he admitted slowly. 'I'm not going to pretend that I'm less ambitious or selfish or fond of money than the next man. Of course I like money—we all do. But values are changing, Tina. Not just your values or my values—but all values. It doesn't really matter if that money is yours or mine or someone else's. All that matters is what is done with it.'

She smiled slowly and very happily.

'And you think that what we have chosen to do with—our money is right?' she said with satisfaction.

'I think,' Charles said deliberately, 'that to buy new life in a world so tragically full of death is the most exciting and romantic and wonderful thing that can happen to anyone.'

There was a long silence. Then she said with a sigh:

'Charles, I'm so happy.'

'Yes, so am I.'

'I can even think of Philip Collier without bitterness now.'

He moved slightly.

'You still haven't told me his place in the story. You weren't in love with him or married to him some time or anything, were you?'

'Charles, how ridiculous! Of course not. It was just that

he recognised me, realised that I had claimed money which wasn't mine, and—and proposed to blackmail me.'

'Swine,' said Charles without heat.

'Charles, he's dead now.'

'Yes,' he agreed thoughtfully. 'As you said—like a judgment.'

She smiled faintly and murmured:

'You're not superstitious, are you?'

'No. Only in so far as I think *something* would have brought you half-way across the world to me, even if it hadn't been your own criminal tendencies,' he told her teasingly.

She laughed softly.

'It's funny—I remember now—that night I left America, and the lights of New York were slipping away behind us, I thought—"I'm like the girl in all the fairy stories, setting out into the world alone. A new life, even a new identity. Where will my wanderings take me?"'

He looked down at her and smiled as she lay there in the circle of his arm.

'And I think,' he said, 'that you are satisfied with the place to which they brought you.'

Harlequin's
Collection
EDITIONS OF 1979

YESTERDAY'S LOVE
FOR ALL YOUR TOMORROWS

You relive your love in memories. Letters tied in blue ribbon...roses pressed between the pages of a book... keepsakes of a romance that will never be forgotten.

A great love story has a different kind of timelessness. It can be cherished in memory, but it can also come alive over and over again. Harlequin proved that three years ago, when we introduced the first 100 Collections—outstanding novels, chosen from two decades of beautiful love stories. Stories that are still treasured by the women who read them.

Harlequin's Collection 162 1.25
MARGERY HILTON
Young Ellis

Now we are bringing you the Harlequin's Collection editions of 1979. Best-selling romantic novels that were written from the heart, giving them a brilliance that the passage of time cannot dim. Like a lovingly crafted family heirloom or a gift from someone you love, these stories will have a special personal significance. Because when you read them today, you'll relive love. A love that will last, for all your tomorrows.

$**1.25** each

Choose from this list of classic Collection editions

Relive a great romance...
Harlequin's Collection 1979
Complete and mail this coupon today!

Harlequin Reader Service

In U.S.A.
MPO Box 707
Niagara Falls, N.Y. 14302

In Canada
649 Ontario St.
Stratford, Ontario, N5A 6W2

Please send me the following Harlequin's Collection novels. I am enclosing my check or money order for $1.25 for each novel ordered, plus 49¢ to cover postage and handling.

☐ 152	☐ 161	☐ 169
☐ 153	☐ 162	☐ 170
☐ 154	☐ 163	☐ 171
☐ 155	☐ 164	☐ 172
☐ 156	☐ 165	☐ 173
☐ 158	☐ 166	☐ 174
☐ 159	☐ 167	☐ 175
☐ 160	☐ 168	☐ 176

Number of novels checked @ $1.25 each = $ _____

N.Y. and N.J. residents add appropriate sales tax $ _____

Postage and handling $ _____ .49

TOTAL $ _____

NAME_____
(Please Print)

ADDRESS _____

CITY _____

STATE/PROV. _____

ZIP/POSTAL CODE_____

Offer expires December 31, 1979   ROM 2290

And there's still *more* love in

Yes!

Six more spellbinding
romantic stories every month
by your favorite authors.
Elegant and sophisticated tales of
love and love's conflicts.

Let your imagination be swept away to
exotic places in search of adventure,
intrigue and romance. Get to
know the warm, true-to-life
characters. Share the special
kind of miracle that
love can be.